Richard Whately

Easy Lessons on Reasoning

Richard Whately

Easy Lessons on Reasoning

ISBN/EAN: 9783337387129

Printed in Europe, USA, Canada, Australia, Japan

Cover: Foto ©Andreas Hilbeck / pixelio.de

More available books at **www.hansebooks.com**

EASY LESSONS

ON

REASONING.

REPRINTED FROM "THE SATURDAY MAGAZINE."

NEW EDITION.

TORONTO:

COPP, CLARK & CO.

1872.

PREFACE.

The subject treated of in the following pages is one which has not usually been introduced into the course of elementary studies for young persons of all classes.

It is supposed by some, that the difference between a better and a worse reasoner depends either wholly on *natural ability*, or on that combined with *practice*, or on each man's greater or less proficiency in the *subjects* he is treating of.

And others again consider a systematic study of the principles of Reasoning as suitable only to a few persons of rare endowments, and of a peculiar turn of mind; and to those only in an advanced stage of their education.

That this branch of study is requisite for all, and is attainable by all, and presents not, necessarily, any greater difficulties than the rudiments of Arithmetic, Geometry, and Grammar,— all this cannot be so well evinced in any other way as by *experiment*. If the perusal of these Lessons, or of the half of them, fail to satisfy on this point any tolerably attentive reader, it is not likely he would be convinced by any distinct argument to the same effect that could be offered.

The work has very little claim to novelty, except as to the simplicity and familiarity of its form. But without making any *discovery*, strictly so called, of anything previously altogether unknown, it is possible—since "discovery" is a *relative* word— to be, practically a discoverer, by bringing within the reach of thousands some important branch of knowledge of which they would otherwise have remained destitute all their lives.

And in regard to the present subject, a familiar introduction to the study is precisely what has been hitherto wanting. The existing treatises upon it may be compared to ships well freighted, but which can only unlade at a few wharfs, carefully constructed, in advantageous situations.   The want is of small boats drawing very little water, which can carry ashore small parcels of the cargo on every part of the coast, and run up into every little creek.

Should the attempt to supply this deficiency prove as successful, as there is reason, from the trial that has been already made (in the *Saturday Magazine*), to hope, an addition by no means unimportant will have been made to the ordinary course of elementary education.

To frame, indeed, a system of rules that should equalize persons of all varieties of capacity, would be a project no less chimerical in this than in other departments of learning.   But it would certainly be a great point gained, if all persons were taught to exercise the reasoning faculty, as well as the natural capacity of each would permit; for there is good reason to suspect, that, in this point, men fail quite as often from want of attention, and of systematic cultivation of their powers, as from natural deficiency.   And it is at least worth trying the experiment, whether *all* may not be, in some degree, trained in the right exercise of a faculty which all in some degree, possess, and which all *must*, more or less, exercise, whether they exercise it well or ill.

It was at one time contemplated to subjoin an *Index* of the technical terms, with brief definitions of them, and references to the Lessons and Sections.   But, on second thoughts, it has been judged best to omit this, and to recommend each student to draw up such an index for himself. It is for *students*, strictly so called,—that is, persons employed in acquiring an elementary knowledge of the subject,—that the work is chiefly designed: and for these no exercise could be devised more calculated to facilitate their study than that of carefully compiling an Index, and also expanding the Table of Contents, so as to give a brief summary of the matter of each Lesson. And this being the case, it would not be any real saving of labor to the learner, to place before him such an Index and Table of Contents already drawn up.

It may be worth while to suggest to the Teacher to put before his pupils, *previously* to their reading each Lesson, some *questions* pertaining to the matter of it, requiring of them answers, oral or written, the best they can think of *without* consulting the book. Next let them read the Lessons, having other questions, such as may lead to any needful explanations, put before them as they proceed. And afterwards let them be examined (introducing numerous *examples* framed by themselves and by the teacher), as to the portion they have learned, in order to judge how far they remember it.

Of these three kinds of questions,—which may be called, i. *Preliminary* questions; ii. questions of *instruction;* and iii. questions of *examination,*—the last alone are, by a considerable portion of Instructors, commonly employed. And the elementary books commonly known as "catechisms," or "books in question and answer," consist in reality of questions of this description.

But the second kind—what is properly to be called instructive questioning—is employed by all who deserve to be reckoned good teachers.

The first kind—the preliminary questioning—is employed (systematically and constantly) but by few. And at first sight it might be supposed by those who have not had experience of it, that it would be likely to increase the learner's difficulties. But if any well-qualified instructor will but carefully and judiciously try the experiment (in teaching any kind of science), he will be surprised to find to how great a degree this exercise of the student's mind on the subject will contribute to his advancement. He will find, that what has been taught in the mode above suggested, will have been learnt in a shorter time, will have been far the more thoroughly understood, and will be fixed incomparably the better in the memory.

CONTENTS.

[To be filled up by the Student.]

Part II.   COMPENDIUM.

EASY LESSONS ON REASONING.

PART I.

ANALYTICAL INTRODUCTION.

LESSON I.

§ 1. Every one is accustomed more or less to employ Reasoning. There is no one that does not occasionally attempt, well or ill, to give a Reason for any opinion he entertains;—to draw Conclusions from what he sees around him,—to support those conclusions by some kind of Arguments, good or bad,—and to answer the arguments brought against him.

Now all these expressions, —"giving a reason "— "drawing a conclusion"—"bringing forward an argument"—relate to one and the same process in the mind, that which is properly called " Reasoning." And the same may be said of several other expressions also ; such as "inferring" or "drawing an inference,"—"proving a point,"—"establishing a conclusion,"—"refuting an argument," &c. All these expressions, and some others besides, have reference, as we have said, to the process of Reasoning.

§ 2. And this process, it is important to observe, is, in *itself*, universally the *same;* however different the subject-matter of our reasoning may be, on different occasions.

The same is the case with Arithmetic. We may have to add or subtract, multiply or divide certain numbers, either of Pounds-sterling, or of men, or of bushels of corn, &c., but though these are very different things, the *arithmetical-process itself*, in each of the operations, respectively, is always the same. For instance, to "multiply" always means to take one number a certain number of times; whether it be men or miles, or days, that we are numbering.

So it is also with Grammar. The Nouns and Verbs and other Parts of Speech that Grammar treats of, may relate to very different subjects, and may be found in various kinds of Compositions; such as works of Science, History, Poetry, &c., but the rules of Grammar are the same in all.

So also the art of Writing (and the same may be said of Printing) is in itself the same, however different may be the kinds of subject-matter it is employed on.

Now the same is the case (as has been above said) with Reasoning. We may be employed in reasoning on human affairs, or on Mathematics, or on Natural-history or Chemistry, or other subjects widely different from each other. But in every case the Reasoning-process is, in itself, the same.

§ 3. Any Debate [or Disputation,] when you are endeavouring to bring others over to your opinion, is *one* of the occasions on which Reasoning is employed; and the word "arguing" is by some persons understood as having reference *only* to cases where there is a *dispute* between those who are maintaining opposite opinions. But this is a mistake. At least, it is a mistake to suppose that the use of "Arguments"—if we understand by that, the use of Reasoning—is confined to the case of *disputes;* or even that this is the *principal* employment of it. There is no set of men less engaged in dispute and controversy than Mathematicians; who are the most constantly occupied in Reasoning. They establish all their propositions by the most exact proofs; so complete as not even to admit of any dispute.

And in all other subjects likewise, a sensible man, when he wishes to make up his mind on any question will always seek for some sufficient "Reason" [or "Argument"] on which to found his conclusion.

Thus, a Judge, before whom any case is tried is occupied in weighing the Arguments on both sides, that are brought forward by the respective Advocates. He (no less than they) is engaged in Reasoning; though the Advocates are *disputing* and the Judge is not.

A Physician, again, reasons from what he has read, and heard, and seen, in order to draw his conclusions on medical questions;—a Statesman, in political questions;—a Merchant, in mercantile matters; and so, of the rest.

§ 4. But when any dispute does take place, between persons of opposed opinions, it may be observed that the worst educated—those who are the most unskilful in reasoning, or in clearly expressing their reasons,—are almost always the most apt to grow angry, and to revile each other, and quarrel.

And even when they do not give way to anger, they usually, after a long discussion, part, without distinctly understanding what the difference between them really consists in; neither of them having clearly expressed his own meaning, or fully understood the other's.

Indeed it often happens that two persons who are disputing, do, in reality, disagree much less in their opinions, than they themselves imagine : or, perhaps not at all. And hence it is that the word "misunderstanding" has come to signify, a *quarrel;* because quarrels so often arise from men's not clearly understanding each other's meaning.

Again, it often happens that a person not without good sense, will give such weak and absurd reasons for his opinion, even when it is a right one, that instead of convincing others, he will even produce an opposite effect.

§ 5. In order to avoid such inconveniences, and to conduct the process of Reasoning as clearly, as correctly, and as easily, as is possible, it is a great advantage to lay down accurate explanations of the *principles* on which Reasoning proceeds, and to employ for the purpose a technical *language*; that is, a regularly-formed set of expressions, distinctly, defined, and agreed on ; and to establish certain plain simple *rules*, founded on, and expressed in, this technical language.

Even in the common mechanical arts, something of a technical language is found needful for those who are learning or exercising them. It would be a very great inconvenience, even to a common carpenter, not to have a precise, well-understood *name* for each of the several operations he performs, such as chiseling, sawing, planing,

&c., and for the several tools [or instruments] he works with. And if we had not such words as Addition, Subtraction, Multiplication, Division, &c., employed in an exactly defined sense, and also fixed rules for conducting these and other arithmetical processes, it would be a tedious and uncertain work, to go through even such simple calculations as a child very soon learns to perform with perfect ease. And after all, there would be a fresh difficulty in making other persons understand clearly the correctness of the calculations made.

You are to observe, however, that technical language and rules, if you would make them really useful, must be not only *distinctly understood*, but also learnt, and *remembered* as familiarly as the Alphabet; and employed *constantly*, and with scrupulous *exactness*. Otherwise, technical language will prove an encumbrance instead of an advantage; just as a suit of clothes would be, if, instead of putting them on and *wearing* them, you were to carry them about in your hand.

§ 6. It has been accordingly found advantageous, in what relates to the Reasoning-process, (as well as in the case of mechanical operations, and of calculations,) to lay down explanations, and rules, and technical terms; answering to those of Arithmetic, Grammar, and other branches of study.

And the technical terms and rules of Grammar, are not at all shorter, or easier to be understood and remembered, than those pertaining to the present subject.

You may perhaps meet with treatises professing much more than what we here propose;—with works pretending to teach the right use of "Reason;" (not Reason*ing* or "Argumentation" merely, but the whole of the *Human Intellect;*) and giving rules for forming a judgment on every question than can arise, and for arriving at all truths in any subject whatever. But such pretensions, however high-sounding and attractive, are fanciful and empty. One might as well profess to teach the "right use of the bodily-organs," and to lay down a system of rules that should instruct a man in all manual arts and bodily exercises at once.

If you do but teach a person to ride, or to draw, or to spin, &c., something is gained; but if you should profess to lay down a system of rules to teach *all these at once,* and also the business of a shipwright, and a musician, and a watchmaker, and everything else that is done by means of the bodily organs, you would teach, in reality, nothing at all.

And so it is on all subjects. It is better to undertake even a little, that it is possible to accomplish, than to make splendid professions, which can only lead to disappointment.

After all, indeed, it cannot be expected, that, in Reasoning, any more than in other mental exercises, men of very unequal degrees of intelligence should be brought to the same level. Nor is it to be expected, that men will always be brought to an agreement in their conclusions. Different men will have received different information respecting facts; or will be variously biassed, more or less, by their early prejudices, their interests, or their feelings.

But still, there is something gained, if they are taught in respect of the Reasoning-process itself, how to proceed rightly and to express themselves clearly; and if when they do not agree, they can be brought at least to understand wherein they differ, and to state distinctly, what is "the point at issue" (as it is called) between them; that is, what is the real question to be decided.

And it is just so, in the case of Arithmetic also. Two persons may differ in their statements of an Account, from their setting out with some difference in the *numbers* each puts down;—in the *Items* (as it is called) of the Account. And no rules of Arithmetic can prevent such a difference as this. But it is something gained if they are guarded (as arithmetical rules do guard us) against differences arising out of errors in the *calculation* itself.

LESSON II.

§ 1. We have said that in all subjects, and on all occasions, the Reasoning-process is in itself the same   Whether you are occupied in *refuting* an opponent, or in conveying *instruction,* or in satisfying your own mind on any point,— and again, whatever kind of subject-matter it is that you are engaged on, in all cases, as far as you are (in the strict sense of the word) *reasoning,*—that is, employing Argument—it is one and the same process (as far as it is *correctly* conducted) that is going on in your own mind.

And what this process is, must be the next point to be inquired into.

Although (as has been said) all men do occasionally reason, they are often, at the time, as *unconscious* of it as of the circulation of their blood, and of the various other processes that may be going on within the body.   And even when they do, knowingly and designedly, use arguments, or are listening to those of another, they will often be as much at a loss to explain *why* one argument appears to them strong, and another less strong, and another utterly worthless, as if the whole were merely a matter of *taste;* like their preference of one prospect, or one piece of music to another.

In order, then, to obtain correct rules for forming a judgment on this subject, and clear expressions for explaining such judgment to others, it is necessary to *analyse,*— as it is called,—that is, take to pieces) the Reasoning-process.   And for that purpose, we should begin by examining the most plain, short, and simple arguments, and enquiring on what it is that their *validity* [or conclusiveness] depends; examining also, some of those apparent-arguments which are *not* valid, and therefore not, in reality, arguments at all; though they are often passed off for them, as counterfeit coin is for genuine.

§ 2. You will perceive, on examination, that what is called a "Conclusion,"—that is, a proposition proved by Argument,—is drawn, in reality, from *two* other Propositions.   And these are called its "Premises;" from their being (in natural order) *"premised"* or put before it.

At first sight, indeed, some might suppose that a Conclusion may follow from one Premise alone.   For it happens, oftener than not, that only one is *expressed.* But in this case, there is always another Premise *understood,* and which is suppressed, from its being supposed to be fully admitted.

That this is the case, may easily be made evident by supposing that suppressed Premise to be *denied ;* which will at one destroy the force of the Argument.   For instance, if any one, from perceiving that "the World exhibits marks of design," infers [or concludes] that " it had an intelligent Maker," he will easily perceive, on reflection, that he must have had in his mind another Premise also, namely, that "whatever exhibits marks of design had an intelligent maker:" since if this last proposition were *denied*, the other would prove nothing.   It is true, that in some cases one proposition implies another by the very signification of the words, to every one that understands those words; as "negroes are men ; therefore they are rational-beings," now, " rational-being" is *implied* in the very *name* "man." And such examples as this have led some people into the idea that we reason— or that we may reason—from a single Premise.   But take such a case as this; some fossil-animal is discovered, which Naturalists conclude to have been a "ruminant," from its "having horns on the skull."   Now the laborers who dug up the skeleton could not draw this inference; supposing they were ignorant of the general law, that "all horned animals are ruminant:"—and they *might* be thus ignorant, though using the name "horned animal," in the same sense as the Naturalist : for the *name* itself does not *imply* "ruminant," as a part of its signification ; and again, a Naturalist at a distance, who *knew* the general law, but who had heard only an imperfect account of the skeleton, and did not know whether it was horned or not, would be equally unable to draw the inference.   In all cases of what is properly called "Argument," there must be *two* premises assumed, whether they are both *expressed* or not.

§ 3. Such an argument as the above, when all the three propositions are stated at full length, and in their natural order, is called a "Syllogism."   And this is the form in which all correct reasoning, on whatever subject, may be exhibited.

When one of the Premises is suppressed [or *understood*], which, for brevity's sake, is usually the case, the argument is called, in technical language, an " Enthymeme;" a name derived from the Greek, and denoting

that there is something left out, which is to be *supposed*
[or understood] as being well-known.

It is to be observed, that, when an argument, stated in
this last form, is met by opponents, their objection will
sometimes lie against the *assertion itself* that is made;
sometimes, against its *force* as an argument.   They will
say either, "I deny what you *assume*," or "I admit, indeed,
what you say, but I deny that it *proves* your conclusion."
For instance, in the example above, an atheist may be
conceived either denying* that the World does exhibit
marks of design, or again, denying† that it *follows* from
thence that it must have had an intelligent Maker.

Now you are to observe, that these are not in reality
objections of different kinds.   The only difference is, that,
in the one case, the *expressed* Premise is denied; in the
other, the *suppressed* Premise.   For the *force* as an argu-
men, of either Premise, depends on the other Premise.
If either be denied, the other proves nothing.   If both
be admitted, the Conclusion regularly drawn from them,
must be admitted.

§ 4. It makes no difference in respect of the sense of
an argument, whether the Conclusion be placed last or
first; provided you do but clearly mark out what *is* the
Conclusion.

When it is placed last (which is accounted the natural
order), it is designated by one of those conjunctions
called "*illative*," such as "therefore,"—"thence,"—"consequently."

When the Conclusion is put first, the Premise is usually
called the "Reason;" and this is designated (whether it
come last or first) by one of the conjunctions called
"*causal*," such as "since,"—"because," &c.

And here it is to be observed, that each of these sets
of conjunctions have also another sense; being used to
denote, respectively, sometimes "Premise and Conclusion,"—sometimes "Cause and Effect."   And much error
and perplexity have often been occasioned by not attending to this distinction.

---

* As many of the ancient atheists did.
† As most of the modern atheists do.

When I say "this ground is rich; because the trees on it are flourishing;" or again, when I express the same sense in a different form, saying, "the trees on this ground are flourishing, and therefore it must be rich," it is plain that I am employing these conjunctions to denote merely the *connexion of Premise and Conclusion;* or (in other words) I am implying that the one may be *inferred* from the other. For it is evident, that the flourishing of the trees is not the *cause* of the ground's fertility, but only the cause of my *believing* it. The richness of the soil *follows as an inference* from the luxuriance of the trees; which luxuriance *follows as an effect* [or, *natural consequence*] from the richness of the soil.

But, if again, I say, "the trees flourish because the ground is rich," or (which is the same in sense) "the ground is rich, and consequently [or therefore] the trees flourish,' I am using the very same conjunction in a different sense; namely, to denote, the *Connexion of Cause and Effect.* For in this case, the luxuriance of the trees being a thing evident to the eye, would not need to be *proved;* and every one would understand that I was only *accounting for it.*

§ 5. But again, there are many cases also in which the *Cause* is employed as an *Argument*, to prove the existence of its effect. So that the Conclusion which *follows*, as an *Inference*, from the Premise is also an Effect which *follows naturally* from that same Premise as its Cause.

This is the kind of argument which is chiefly employed when we are reasoning about the *future :* as for instance when, from favorable or unfavorable weather, any one infers that the crops are likely to be abundant, or to be scanty.

In such cases, the *Cause* and the *Reason* [or Proof] coincide ; the favorable weather being at once the cause of the good harvest, and the cause *of our expecting it.*

And this circumstance contributes to men's often confounding together "Cause" and—what is strictly called— "Reason;" and to their overlooking the different senses of such words as "therefore," "thence," " consequently," &c., and again, of such words as "because," "inasmuch as,' &c., and also, of the words "follow," "consequence,"

and several others ; which have all of them that double
meaning which has just been explained.

LESSON III.

§ 1. In such an argument as that in the example
above given, (in § 2, Lesson ii.) it is clearly impossible
for any one who admits both Premises to avoid admitting
the Conclusion.   If you admit that " Whatever exhibits
marks of design had an intelligent Maker," and also
that "the world exhibits marks of design," you cannot
escape the Conclusion that "the world had an intelligent
Maker."

Or again, if I say "All animals with horns on the head
are ruminant; the Elk has horns on the head ; therefore
it is ruminant;" it is impossible to conceive any one's
doubting the truth of the Conclusion, supposing he does
but allow the truth of each Premise.

A man may perhaps deny, or doubt, and require proof,
that all animals thus horned do ruminate.   Nay it is
conceivable that he may even not clearly understand what
"ruminant," means, or he may have never heard of an
"Elk;" but still it will not be the less clear to him that
supposing these Premises granted, the Conclusion must
be admitted.

And even if you suppose a case where one or both of
the Premises shall be manifestly false and absurd, this
will not alter the *conclusiveness* of the Reasoning; though
the *conclusion* itself may perhaps be absurd also.   For
instance, "All the Ape-tribe are originally descended from
Reptiles or insects : Mankind are of the Ape-tribe ; therefore Mankind are originally descended from Reptiles or
Insects ; here, every one* would perceive the falsity of
all three of these propositions.   But it is not the less true
that the conclusion *follows* from those premises, and that
if they were true, it would be true also.

§ 2. But it oftens happen that there will be a *seeming*

---

* Except certain French Naturalists.

connexion of certain premises with a conclusion which does not really follow from them, although, to the inattentive or unskilful, the argument will appear to be valid. And this is most especially likely to occur when such a seeming argument [or Fallacy] is dressed up in a great quantity of fine-sounding words, and is accompanied with much vehemence of assertion, and perhaps with expressions of contempt for anyone who presumes to entertain a doubt on the matter. In a long declamatory speech, especially, it will often happen that almost any proposition at all will be passed off as a proof of any other that does but contain *some of the same words*, by means of strenuous assurances that the proof is complete.

Sometimes again, sound arguments will be distrusted as fallacious; especially if they are not clearly expressed; and the more if the conclusions are such as men are not willing to admit.

And frequently also, when there really is no sound argument, the reader or hearer, though he believes or suspects that there *is* some fallacy, does not know how to detect and explain it.

§ 3. Suppose, for instance, such seeming-arguments as the following to be proposed:—(1.) " Every criminal is deserving of punishment; this man is not a criminal; therefore he is not deserving of punishment :" or again, (2.) "All wise rulers endeavor to civilize the People; Alfred endeavored to civilize the People; therefore he was a wise ruler." There are perhaps some few persons who would not perceive any fallacy in such arguments, even when thus briefly and distinctly stated. And there are probably many who would fail to perceive such a fallacy, if the arguments were enveloped in a cloud of words, and conveyed at great length, in a style of vague indistinct declamation; especially if the conclusions were such as they were disposed to admit. And others again, might perceive, indeed, that there *is* a fallacy, but might be at a loss to explain and expose it.

Now the above examples exactly correspond respectively, with the following; in which the absurdity is manifest :—(1.) " Every tree is a vegetable; grass is not a tree; therefore it is not a vegetable;" and (2.) "all vegetables grow; an animal grows; therefore it is a vegetable." These last examples, I say, correspond exactly (considered in respect of the *reasoning*) with the former ones; the conclusions of which, however *true*, no more follow from the premises than those of the last.

This way of exposing a fallacy by bringing forward a similar one where a manifestly absurd conclusion professes to be drawn from premises that are true, is one which we may often find it needful to employ when addressing persons who have no knowledge of technical rules; and to whom, consequently, we could not speak so as to be understood concerning the principles of Reasoning.

But it is evidently the most convenient, the shortest, and the safest course, to ascertain those principles, and on them to found rules which may be employed as a test in every case that comes before us.

And for this purpose, it is necessary (as has been above said) to analyse the Reasoning process, as exhibited in some valid argument expressed in its plainest and simplest form.

§ 4. Let us then examine and analyse such an example as one of those first given: for instance, "Every animal that has horns on the head is ruminant; the Elk has horns on the head; therefore the Elk is ruminant." It will easily be seen that the validity [or "conclusiveness;" or "soundness"] of the Argument does not at all depend on our conviction of the truth of either of the Premises; or even on our understanding the meaning of them. For if we substitute some unmeaning Symbol (such as a letter of the alphabet) which may stand for anything that may be agreed on — for one of the things we are speaking about, the Reasoning remains the same.

For instance, suppose we say, (instead of "animal that has horns on the head,") "Every X is ruminant;" "the Elk is X; therefore the Elk is ruminant;" the argument is equally valid.

And again, instead of the word "ruminant," let us put the letter "Y:" then the argument "Every X is Y; the Elk is X; therefore the Elk is Y;" would be a valid argument as before.

And the same would be the case if you were to put "Z" for "the Elk:" for the syllogism "Every X is Y; Z is X; therefore Z is Y," is completely valid, whatever you suppose the Symbols, X, Y, and Z to stand for.

Any one may try the experiment, by substituting for X, Y, and Z, respectively, any words he pleases; and he will find that if he does but preserve the same *form* of expression, it will be impossible to admit the truth of the Premises, without admitting also the truth of the Conclusion.

§ 5. And it is worth observing here that nothing is so likely to lead to that—very common, though seemingly strange—error, of supposing ourselves to understand distinctly what in reality we understand but very imperfectly, or not at all, as the want of attention to what has been just explained.

A man reads—or even writes—many pages perhaps, of an argumentative work, in which one or more of the terms employed convey nothing distinct to his mind: and yet he is liable to overlook this circumstance from finding that he clearly understands the *Arguments*.

He may be said, in one sense, to *understand what he is reading;* because he can perfectly follow the *train of Reasoning,* itself. But, *this,* perhaps, he might equally well do, if he were to substitute for one of the words employed, X, or Z, or any other such unknown Symbol; as in the examples above.

But a man will often confound together, the *understanding of the Arguments,* in themselves, and the *understanding of the words employed,* and of the nature of the things those words denote.

It appears then that valid Reasoning, when regularly expressed, has its validity [or conclusiveness] made evident from the mere *form of the expression* itself, independently of any regard to the sense of the words.

§ 6. In examining this form, in such an example as that just given, you will observe, that in the first premise ("X is Y,") it is assumed universally of the *Class* of things (whatever it may be) which "X" denotes, that "Y" may be affirmed of them: and in the other Premise, "Z is X") that "Z" (whatever it may stand for) is *referred* to that Class, as *comprehended* in it. Now it is evident that whatever is said for the *whole* of a class may be said of anything that is comprehended [or "included," or "con-

B

tained,"] in that Class: so that we are thus authorized to say (in the conclusion) that "Z" is "Y."

Thus also in the example first given, having assumed universally, of the Class of "Things which exhibit marks of design," that they "had an intelligent maker," and then, in the other Premise, having referred "The world" to that Class, we conclude that it may be asserted of "The world" that "it had an intelligent maker."

And the process is the same when anything is *denied* of a whole Class. We are equally authorized to deny the same of whatever is comprehended under that Class. For instance, if I say, "No liar is deserving of trust; this man is a liar; therefore he is not deserving of trust:" I here deny "deserving of trust," of the whole Class denoted by the word "liar;" and then I refer "this man" to that Class; whence it follows that "deserving of trust" may be denied of him.

§ 7. This argument also will be as manifestly valid, if (as in the former case) you substitute for the words which have a known meaning, any undetermined symbols, such as letters of the alphabet. "No X is Y; Z is X; therefore Z is not Y," is as perfect a syllogism as the other, with the affirmative conclusion.

To such a form all valid arguments whatever may be reduced: and accordingly the principle according to which they are constructed, is to be regarded as the UNIVERSAL PRINCIPLE OF REASONING.

It may be stated, as a general Maxim, thus: "Whatever is said, whether affirmatively, or negatively," [or "whatever is affirmed or denied"] "of a whole Class may be said in like manner," [that is "affirmed in the one case, and denied in the other,"] "of everything comprehended under that Class."

Simple as this principle is, the whole process of Reasoning is embraced in it. Whenever we establish any Conclusion,—that is, show that one thing may allowably be affirmed, or be denied, of another—this is always in reality done by referring that other to some Class of which such affirmation or denial can be made.

The longest series of arguments, when fully unfolded, step by step, will be found to consist of nothing but a repetition of the same simple operation here described. But this circumstance is apt to be overlooked, on account of the *brevity* with which we usually express ourselves. A Syllogism, such as those in the examples above, is seldom given at full length ; but is usually abridged into an "Enthymeme."* (See Lesson ii. § 3.) And moreover what is called *"an argument,"* is very often not *one* argument, but *several* compressed together; sometimes into a single sentence. As when one says: "The adaptation of the instinct of suction in young animals to the supply of milk in the parent, and to the properties of the Atmosphere as well as other like marks of design, show that the world must have had an intelligent maker." For most men are excessively impatient of the tedious formality of stating at full length anything that they are already aware of, and could easily understand by a slight hint.

LESSON IV.

§ 1. We have seen that when an argument is stated in the regular form (as in the foregoing examples), which is what is properly called a "Syllogism," the validity [or conclusiveness] of the reasoning is manifest from the mere form of the expression itself, without regard to the sense of the words ; so that if letters or other such arbitrary anmeaning Symbols, be substituted, the force of the argument will be not the less evident. Whenever this is not the case, the supposed argument is either sophistical and unreal, or else may be reduced (without any alteration of its meaning) into the above form : in which form, the general Maxim that has been laid down will apply to it.

What is called an unsound [or fallacious] argument (that is an *apparent*-argument which is in reality *none*) cannot, of course, be reduced into such a form. But when it is stated in the form most nearly approaching to this that is possible, and especially when unmeaning symbols (such as letters), are substituted for words that have a meaning, its fallaciousness becomes evident from its want of conformity to the above Maxim.

---

* That is, an argument with one of the Premises understood.

§ 2. Let us take the Example formerly given: "Every criminal is deserving of punishment ; this man is not a criminal; therefore he is not deserving of punishment;" this, if stated in letters, would be, "Every X is Y ; Z is not X ; therefore Z is not Y." Here the term ("Y") "deserving of punishment" is affirmed universally of the Class ("X") "Criminal;" and it might therefore, according to the Maxim, be affirmed of anything comprehended under that Class ; but in the instance before us, *nothing* is mentioned as comprehended under that Class ; only "this man" ("Z") is *excluded* from that Class. And although what is affirmed of a whole Class may be *affirmed* of anything which that Class does contain, we are not authorized to *deny* it of whatever is *not* so contained. For it is evident that what is truly affirmed of a Class, may be applicable *not only* to that Class, but also to *other things* besides.

For instance, to say that "every tree is a vegetable" does not imply that "nothing else is a vegetable." And so also, to say that "every criminal is deserving of punishment" does not imply that "no others are deserving of punishment:" for however *true* this is, it *has not been asserted* in the proposition before us. And in analysing an argument we are to dismiss all consideration of what *might* have been asserted with truth, and to look only to what *actually* is laid down in the Premises.

It is evident, therefore, that such an apparent-argument as the above does not comply with the rule [or Maxim] laid down ; nor can it be so stated as to comply with it ; and it is consequently invalid.

§ 3. Again, let us take another of the examples formerly given; "All wise rulers endeavour to civilize the People; Alfred endeavoured to civilize the People ; therefore he was a wise ruler." The parallel example to this was, "All vegetables grow; an animal grows ; therefore it is a vegetable." And each of these, if stated in Symbols, would stand thus: every "Y is X," [or the thing denoted by Y is comprehended under the Class for which X stands,] "Z is X; therefore Z is Y."

Now in such an example, the quality of "growing" ["X"] is, in one Premise, affirmed universally of "vegetable," ["Y"], and it *might* therefore have been affirmed of anything that can be referred to the Class of "vegetable" as comprehended therein : but then, there is *nothing* referred to that Class in the other Premise; only, the same thing which had been affirmed of the Class "vegetable," is again affirmed of another Class, " animals" (Z); whence nothing can be inferred.

Again, take such an instance as this ; " Fruit is produced in England ; dates are fruit; therefore dates are produced in England." Here "produced in England" is affirmed of "fruit," but not *universally ;* for every one would understand you to be speaking not of *" all* fruit," but of *"some* fruit," as being produced in England. So that, expressed in Symbols, the apparent-argument would stand thus: "Some X is Y ; Z is X ; therefore Z is Y ;" in which you may see that the Rule has not been complied with ; since that which has been affirmed not of the *whole* of a certain Class, [or, not *universally*] but only of *part* of it, cannot on that ground be affirmed of whatever is contained under that Class.

§ 4. There is an argument against miracles by the well-known Mr. Hume, which has preplexed many persons, and which exactly corresponds to the above. It may be stated thus: "Testimony is a kind of evidence more likely to be false than a miracle to be true;" (or, as it may be expressed in other words, we have more reason to expect that a witness should lie, than that a miracle should occur); " the evidence on which the Christian miracles are believed is testimony ; therefore the evidence on which the Christian miracles are believed is more likely to be false than a miracle to be true."

Here it is evident, that what is spoken of in the first of these Premises is, " *some* testimony ;" not "all testimony," [or *any whatever*,] and by " a witness" we understand, *"some* witness," not "*every* witness;" so that this apparent-argument has exactly the same fault as the one above. And you are to observe, that it makes no difference (as to the point now before us) whether the word "*some*" be employed, or a different word, such as "*most*" or "many," if it be in any way said or implied that you are *not* speaking of "*all*." For instance, " *most* birds can fly ; and an ostrich is a bird," proves nothing.

§ 5. In order to understand the more clearly, and to describe the more accurately, the fallaciousness of such seeming arguments as those of which we have just given examples, and also, the conclusiveness of the sound arguments, it will be necessary to explain some technical words and phrases which are usually employed for that purpose. This is no less needful (as was remarked in Lesson i.) than for an Artisan to have certain fixed and suitable names for the several instruments he works with, and the operations he performs.

The word "*Proposition*" (which we have already had occasion to use) signifies "a Sentence in which something is *said*—[or predicated]—that is *affirmed* or *denied*—of another." That which is spoken of, is called the "*Subject*" of the Proposition : and that which is said of it, is called the "*Predicate;*" and these two are called the "*Terms*" of the Proposition: from their being (in natural order) the *extremes* [or boundaries] of it.

You are to observe, that it matters not whether each of these Terms consist of *one word*, or of several. For whether a Proposition be short or long, there must always be in it, *one*—and but one—thing of which you are speaking; which is called (as has been just said) the Subject of it : and there must be (in any *one* Proposition) one thing,— and only one—that is affirmed or denied of that Subject : and this which we thus affirm or deny of the other, is called—whether it be one word or more—the Predicate.

§ 6. You are to observe also, that though (in our language) the Subject is usually placed *first*, this order is not at all essential. For instance, "it is wholesome to rise early," or "to rise early is wholesome," or "rising early is wholesome," are only three ways of expressing the same Proposition. In each of these expressions "rising early," (or "to rise early," for these are only two forms of the Infinitive) is what you are speaking of ; and "wholesome" is what you say [or *predicate*] of it.

When we state a proposition in *arbitrary Symbols*, as "X is Y," it is understood that the first term ("X") stands for the subject, and the last ("Y") for the Predicate. But when we use terms that are *significant*, [or, have a meaning] we must judge by the sense of the words *which* it is that is the Subject, and which the Predicate; that is we must ask ourselves the question, "What am I speaking of; and what am I saying of it?"

For instance; "Great is Diana of the Ephesians;" here "great" is evidently the Predicate. Again, "Thou art the man;" and "Thou hast given occasion to the enemies of the Lord to blaspheme;" by asking yourself the above question, you will perceive, that in the former of these examples, "Thou" is the Predicate, and in the latter, the Subject.*

§ 7. That which expresses the affirmation or denial, is called the "*Copula.*" For instance, if I say, "X is Y," or " X is not Y," in each of these examples, "X," is the Subject, and "Y" the Predicate; and the Copula is the word "*is*" in the one, and "is not," in the other.

And so it is, in sense, though not always in expression, in every Proposition. For either the Affirmative-copula, "is" or the Negative-copula, "is not," must be always, in every Proposition, either expressed in those words, or implied in some other expression.

Any sentence which does not do this—in short, which does not *affirm* or *deny*—is not a *Proposition*. For instance, of these sentences, "Are your brothers gone to school?" "They are not gone;" "Let them go," the second alone is a Proposition [or "Assertion"]; the first being a *Question*, and the last a *Command*, or Request.

LESSON V.

§ 1. We have seen that in every Proposition there is something that is spoken of; which is called the subject; and something that you affirm or deny of it; which is called the Predicate. And it is evidently of great importance to understand and express clearly, in each Proposition, whether the Predicate is said of the *whole* of the Subject, or only of *part* of it:—in other words, whether it is *predicated* "*universally,*" or "*particularly,*" [*partially.*]

---

* The Predicate is the *emphatic* word or words in each proposition, and marked as such, by the voice, in speaking, and sometimes by Italics or underscoring in writing; as you may perceive from the examples above.

If, for instance, I say, or am understood to imply, that "*all* testimony is unworthy of credit," this is a very different assertion from saying or implying, merely that "*some* testimony is unworthy of credit." The former of these is called a "*Universal*" Proposition ; the Subject of it being *taken universally*, as standing for *anything and everything* that the term is capable of being applied to in the same sense. And a term so taken is said (in technical language) to be "*distributed*." The latter of the two is called a "*Particular Proposition;*" the Subject being *taken particularly*, as standing only for *part* of the things signified by it: and the Term is then said to be "*undistributed*."

The technical word "distributed" (meaning what some writers express by the phrase "taken universally" is used, as you perceive, in a sense far removed from what it bears in ordinary language. But,—for that very reason,—it is the less likely to lead to mistakes and confusion. And when once its technical sense is explained, it is easily remembered. When I say "birds come from eggs," and again, "birds sing," I mean, in the former proposition, "all birds" [or "every bird"]; in the latter proposition I mean, not "*all*," but "*some*" birds. In the former case the term "birds" is said to be "distributed;" in the latter, "undistributed." You must be careful also to keep in mind the technical sense (already explained) of the word "*particular*." In ordinary discourse, we often speak of "this *particular* person" or thing; meaning "this *individual*." But the technical sense is different. If I say, "this city is large" the Proposition is not "Particular," but is equivalent to a *Universal;* since I am speaking of the *whole* of the Subject; which is "*this single city*." But "*some* city is large," or "some cities are large" is a particular proposition;. because the Subject, "*city*," is taken not *universally*, but *partially*.

The distinction between a "Universal" proposition and a "Particular," is (as I have said) very important in Reasoning; because, as has been already remarked, although what is said of the *whole* of a Class may be said of anything contained in that Class, the Rule does not apply when something is said merely of a *part* of a Class. (See the example "X is Y" in § 3 of the preceding Lesson.)

§ 2. You will have seen that in some of the foregoing examples, the words "all," "every," or "any," which are used to denote the distribution of a Subject, and again, "some," which denotes its non-distribution, are not *expressed*. They are often *understood*, and left to be supplied in the reader's or hearer's mind. Thus, in the last example, "birds sing," evidently means "*some* birds;" and "man is mortal" would be understood to mean "*every* man."

A Proposition thus expressed, is called "*Indefinite;*" it being left *undetermined* ["undefined"] by the form of expression, whether it is to be considered as Universal or as Particular. And mistakes as to this point will often given a plausible air to fallacies; such as that in the last lesson (§ 4) respecting "Testimony."

But it is plain, that every proposition must in reality *be* either Universal or Particular [that is, must have its Subject intended to be understood as distributed, or, as not distributed]; though we may not be told *which* of the two is meant.

And this is called, in technical language, the distinction of Propositions according to their "Quantity;" namely, into Universal and Particular. "Every X is Y" and "some X is Y," are propositions differing from each other in their "quantity," and in nothing else.

§ 3. But the *Predicate* of a proposition, you may observe, has no such sign as "all" or "some," affixed to it, which denote, when affixed to the *Subject*, the distribution or non-distribution of that term. And yet it is plain that each Term of a proposition—whether Subject or Predicate —must always be meant to stand either for the whole, or for part, of what is signified by it;—in other words,— must really *be* either distributed or undistributed. But this depends, in the case of the Predicate, not on the "quantity" of the proposition, but on what is called its "*Quality;*" that is, its being *Affirmative* or *Negative*. And the invariable rule (which will be explained presently) is, that the Predicate of a Negative-proposition is distributed and the Predicate of an Affirmative, undistributed.

When I say "X is Y," the term "Y" is considered as standing for *part* of the things to which it is applicable;

in other words, is "undistributed." And it makes no difference as to this point whether I say "*all* X," or "*some* X is Y." The *Predicate* is equally undistributed in both cases; the only thing denoted by the signs "all" or "some," being the distribution or non-distribution of the *Subject.*

If, on the other hand, I say, "X is not Y," whether meaning, that "*No* X is Y," or that "*some* X is not Y," in either case "Y," is distributed.

§ 4. The reason of this rule you will understand, by considering, that a term which may with truth be affirmed of some other, may be such as would *also* apply equally well, and in the same sense, to *something else besides* that other. Thus, it is true that "all iron is a metal," although the term "metal" is equally applicable to gold, copper, &c., so that you could not say with truth that "all metal is iron," or that "iron, *and that only*, is a metal." For the term "iron" is of narrower extent than the term "metal;" which is affirmed of it.

So that, in the above proposition, what we have been comparing, are the *whole* of the term "iron," and *part* of the term "metal;" which latter term, consequently, is undistributed.

And this explanation applies to every affirmative proposition. For though it *may so happen* that the Subject and the Predicate may be of equal extent [or "*equivalent;*" or as some express it, "convertible"] so that the Predicate which is affirmed of that Subject could *not* have been affirmed of *anything else,* this is not *implied in the expression* of the proposition itself.

In the assertions, for instance, that " every equilateral triangle is equiangular," and that "any two triangles which have all the sides of one equal to all the sides of the other, each to each, are of equal areas," it is not implied that "every equiangular triangle is equilateral," or that "any two triangles of equal areas, have their respective sides equal." This latter, indeed, is not *true:* the one preceding it *is* true: that is, it is true that "every equiangular triangle is equilateral," as well as that "every equilateral triangle is equiangular:" but these are two distinct propositions, and are separately proved in treatises on Geometry."

If it happen to be my object to assert that the Predicate

as well as the Subject of a certain affirmative proposition is to be understood as distributed—and if I say, for instance, "all equilateral triangles, *and no others*, are equiangular,"—I am asserting, in reality, not *one* proposition merely, but *two*. And this is the case whenever the proposition I state is understood (whether from the meaning of the words employed, or from the general drift of the discourse) to imply that the whole of the Predicate is meant to be affirmed of the subject.

Thus, if I say of one number—suppose 100—that it is the Square of another, as 10, then this is understood by every one, from his *knowledge of the nature of numbers*, to imply, what are, in reality, the *two* propositions, that "100 is the Square of 10," and also that "the Square of 10 is 100."

Terms thus related to each other are called in technical language "*convertible*" [or "equivalent"] terms.* But then, you are to observe that when you not only affirm one term of another, but also affirm (or imply) that these *are* "*convertible*" terms, you are making not merely *one* assertion, but *two*.

§ 5. It appears, then, that in affirming that "X is Y," I assert merely that "Y," *either the whole* of it, or *part*, *(it is not declared which)*, is applicable to "X;" [or "comprehends," or "contains" X]. Consequently, if *any* *part* of a certain Predicate be applicable to the Subject, it must be affirmed,—and of course *cannot be denied*—of that Subject. To *deny*, therefore, the Predicate of the Subject, must imply that *no part* of the Predicate is applicable to that Subject; in short, that the *whole* Predicate is denied of that Subject.

You may thus perceive that to assert that "X is *not* Y," is to say that *no part* of the term "Y" is applicable to "X;" (for if *any* part *were* applicable, "Y" could be *affirmed*, and not denied of "X:") in other words, that the *whole* of "Y" is denied of "X;" and that consequently "Y" is "distributed." When I say for instance, "All the men found on that island are sailors of the ship that was

---

* In any language which has a *definite article*—as "*the*" in English,—this denotes that the terms are convertible. In Latin, which has no article, we are left to judge from the context.

wrecked there," this might be equally true whether the
whole crew or only some of them were saved on the
island. To say, therefore, that "the men found on that
island are *not* sailors of the ship," &c., would be to *deny
that any part* of that crew are there; in short, it would
be to say that the whole of that Predicate is *in*applicable
to that subject.

§ 6. And this holds good equally whether the negative
proposition be "universal" or "particular." For to say
that some "X is not Y" (or—which is the same in sense
—that "All X is not Y") is to imply that there is *no
part* of the term "Y" [no part of the class which "Y"
stands *for*] that is applicable to the *whole without exception*, of the term "X;"—in short, that there is *some part*
of the term "X" to which "Y" is wholly inapplicable.

Thus, if I say "some of the men found on that island
are not sailors of the ship that was wrecked there," or, in
other words, "the men found on that island are *not, all
of them*, sailors of the ship," &c., I imply that the term
"sailors," &c., is *wholly* inapplicable to *some* of the "men
on the island;" though it might, perhaps, be applicable
to others of them.

Again if I say "some coin is made of silver," and
"some coin is not made of silver" (or, in other words, that
"all coin is not made of silver") in the former of these
propositions I imply, that in *some portion* (at least) of the
Class of "things made of silver," is found [or compre-
hended] "some coin:" in the latter proposition I imply
that there is "some coin" which is contained in *no* portion
of the Class of "things made of silver;" or (in other words)
which is *excluded* from the *whole* of that Class. So that
the term "made of silver" is distributed in this latter
proposition, and not, in the former.

Hence may be understood the Rule above given, that in
all Affirmative-propositions the Predicate is undistributed
and in all Negative-propositions, is distributed.

The "Subject" is, as we have seen above, distributed
in a Universal-proposition (whether affirmative or negative) and not in a Particular. So that the distribution
or non-distribution of the *Subject* depends on the " *Quantity*" of the proposition, and that of the *Predicate*, on the

LESSON VI.

§ 1. The next thing to be learnt and remembered is the names of the three Terms that occur in a Syllogism. For you will have perceived from the foregoing examples, that there are always *three* terms ; which we have designated by the Symbols X, Y, and Z. Each Syllogism indeed has, in all, three Propositions ; and every Proposition has two Terms ; but in a Syllogism each Term occurs twice; as, "X is Y ; Z is X ; therefore Z is Y."

Of these three Terms then, that which is taken as the *Subject of the Conclusion* ("Z") is called the "*Minor-term;*" the Predicate of the conclusion ("Y") is called the "*Major-term;*" (from its being usually of more *extensive* signification than the "Minor," of which it is predicated;) and the Term ["X"] which is used for establishing the connexion between those two, is thence called the "*Middle-term,*" [or "*medium of proof.*"]

Of these two Premises, that which contains the Major-term, ("X is Y,") is called the "*Major-premise;*" (and it is, properly, and usually, placed *first;* though this order is not essential;) and that which contains the Minor-term ("Z is X") is called the "*Minor-premise.*" And in these two premises, respectively, the Major-term and Minor-term are, each, compared with the Middle-term, in order that, in the Conclusion, they may be compared with each other ; that is, one of them affirmed or denied of the other.

§ 2. Now it is requisite, as you will see, by looking back to the examples formerly given, that, in one or other of the Premises, the Middle-term should be *distributed.* For if each of the terms of the Conclusion had been compared only with *part* of the Middle-term, they would not have been both compared with the *same ;* and nothing could thence be inferred.

Thus, in one of the above examples, when we say "food" (namely, "*some* food,") "is necessary to life," the term "food" is undistributed, as being the Subject of a Particular-proposition ; in other words, we have affirmed the

term "necessary to life," of *part* only, not the *whole*, of
the Class denoted by the term "food;" and again, when
we say "corn is food" the term "food" is again undistributed, (according to the Rule given in the last Lesson),
as being the Predicate of an Affirmative; in other
words, though we have asserted that the term "food" *is*
applicable to "corn," we have not said (nor, as it happens,
is it true) that it is *not applicable* to anything *else;* so
that we have not been taking this term "food" universally,
in either Premise, but, each time, "particularly." And
accordingly nothing follows from those premises.

So also, when it is said, "A wise ruler endeavours to
civilise the People; and Alfred endeavoured to civilise the
People;" [or, "Y is X, and Z is X;"] the Middle-term
is here twice made the Predicate of an Affirmative proposition, and consequently is left undistributed, as in the
former instance; and, as before, nothing follows. For,
(as was formerly observed) we are not authorized to affirm
one term of another, merely on the ground that there is
something which has been affirmed of each of them; as
the term "growing" (in the example formerly given) is
affirmed of "vegetables" and also of "animals."

In each of these cases then, such an apparent argument
is condemned on the ground that it "*has the middle-term
undistributed.*"

§ 3. The other kind of apparent Syllogism formerly
given as an example, is faulty (as was then shown) from
a different cause, and is condemned under a different
title. "Every tree is a vegetable; grass is not a tree,
therefore it is not a vegetable;" or, "Every X is Y; Z
is not X; therefore Z is not Y."

Here, the middle-term "X" is distributed; and that,
not only in one premise, but in both; being made, first,
the subject of a Universal proposition, and again, the
Predicate of a negative. But then, the Major-term,
"Y" which has not been *distributed in the Premise*, is yet
distributed in the Conclusion; being in the *Premise*, the
Predicate of an *Affirmative*, and, in the *Conclusion*, of a
Negative. We have therefore merely compared part of
the term ["Y"] "vegetable" with the Middle-term "Tree;"
["X;"] and this does not authorize our comparing, in the

Conclusion, the *whole* of the same term with [Z] "grass;" which, as was explained above, we must do, if we *deny* the term "grass" of "vegetable."

Nothing therefore follows from the Premises; for it is plain that they would not warrant an *affirmative* Conclusion. To affirm that "grass *is* a vegetable," (or, as one might equally well, that "a house is a vegetable,") because it "is not a tree," would not have even any appearance of Reasoning. No one would pretend to *affirm* one term of another (as Y, of Z) on the ground that it had been affirmed of something ("X") which had been denied of that other.

Such a fallacy as the one we have been above considering, is condemned as having what is called in technical language, an "*illicit process;*" that is an *unauthorised proceeding*, from a term, *un*distributed in the *Premise*, to the same term, *distributed*, in the Conclusion : or, in other words, taking a term *more extensively* in the Conclusion than it had been taken in the Premise; which is, in fact, introducing an additional term.

§ 4. The examples that have been all along given, both of correct-reasoning and of Fallacy, have been, designedly, the *simplest and easiest* that could be framed. And hence, a thoughtless reader, observing that the rules given, and the technical language employed, though not difficult to learn, are yet *less* easy than the examples themselves to which these are applied, may be apt to fancy that his labor has been wasted; and to say, "Why common sense would show any one the soundness of the reasoning, or the unsoundness, in such examples as these, with less trouble than it costs to learn the rules, and the technical terms."

And a beginner of Arithmetic might say the same. For the examples usually set before a learner, are, purposely, such easy questions as he could answer "in his head" (as we say) with less trouble than the arithmetical rules cost him. But then, by learning those rules, *through the means of* such simple examples, he is enabled afterwards to answer, with little difficulty, such arithmetical questions as would be perplexing and laborious, even to a person of superior natural powers, but untaught.

It is the same, in the learning of a foreign Language.

The beginner has to bestow more pains on the transla-
ting of a few simple sentences, than the matter of those
sentences is worth. But in the end, he comes to be able
to read valuable books in the Language, and to converse
with intelligent foreigners, which he could not otherwise
have done.

And so also, in the present case, it will be found, that,
simple·as are the examples given, not only all valid
Reasoning, on whatever subjects, may be exhibited, and
its validity shown, in the form that was first put before
you, but also, most of the Sophistical arguments [Fal-
lacies] by which men are every day misled, on the most
important subjects, may be reduced into the same forms
as those of the examples lately given.

Hume's argument against Miracles as believed on
Testimony, which was explained in a former lesson, is an
instance of this. And numberless others might be given.

§ 5. For example, there is an erroneous notion commonly to be met with, which is founded on a fallacy that
may be thus exhibited as a case of undistributed middle
term: "A man who is indifferent about all religion, is
one who does not seek to force his religion on others;" (for
though this is far from universally *true*, it is commonly
believed;) "this man does not seek to force his religion on
others; therefore he is indifferent to all religion."

Again, as an example of the other kind of fallacy above-
mentioned, the "illicit process" of the Major-term, we may
exhibit in that form the sort of reasoning by which one
may suppose the Priest and the Levite, in the Parable
of the Good Samaritan, to have satisfied themselves that
the poor wounded *stranger* had no claim on them as a
neighbor;—a kind of procedure of which one may find
instances in real life in all times :

"A kinsman or intimate acquaintance has a claim to
our neighborly good-offices : this man, however, is not a
kinsman, &c., therefore he has no claim," &c. Again, "A
Nation which freely admits our goods ought to be allowed
freely to supply us with theirs : but the French do not
freely admit our goods : therefore," &c. Again, "Nations
that have the use of money, and have property in land,
are subject to the evils of avarice, of dishonesty, and of

abject poverty; but savage nations have not the use of money," &c., &c.

And again, " A kind and bountiful landlord ought to be exempted from lawless outrage; but this man is *not* a kind and bountiful landlord; therefore," &c.

It will be found a very useful exercise to select for yourself a number of other arguments, good or bad, such as are commonly to be met with in books or conversation ; and to reduce them to the most regular form they will admit of, in order to try their validity by the foregoing rules.

You must keep in mind, however, (what was said in the first Lesson) that technical terms and rules will be rather an incumbrance than a help, unless you take care not only to understand them thoroughly, but also to learn them so perfectly that they may be as readily and as correctly employed as the names of the most familiar objects around you.

But if you take the trouble to do this *once for all*, you will find that, in the end, much trouble will have been saved. For, the explanations given of such technical-terms and general rules, when thoroughly learnt once, will save you the necessity of going through nearly the *same* explanation, *over and over again*, on each separate occasion.

In short, the advantage of technical-terms is just like what we derive from the use of *any other* Common-terms.*

When, for instance, we have once accurately learnt the definition of a " Circle," or have had fully described to us what sort of creature an "Elephant" is, to say, "I drew a Circle," or "I saw an Elephant," would be sufficiently intelligible, without any need of giving the description or definition at full length, over and over again, on every separate occasion.

LESSON VII.

---

§ 1. We have seen that all sound Reasoning consists in referring that of which we would (in the conclusion) affirm or deny something, to a *Class*, of which that affirmation or

---

* This will be more fully explained in the subsequent Lessons.

denial may be made. Now, the "referring of anything
to a class," means (as you will perceive on looking back
to the examples that have been given) to *affirm of it a
term denoting a Class;* which Term, you will have observed,
is the Middle-term of the Syllogism.

We are next led therefore to inquire what terms may
be affirmatively predicated of what others.

It is plain that a *proper-name,* or any other term that
stands for a *single individual,* cannot be affirmed of
anything except that very individual.   For instance,
"Romulus"—the "Thames"—"England"—"the founder
of Rome"—"this river," &c., denoting each, a *single*
object, are thence called *"Singular terms:"* and each of
them can be affirmed of that single object only, and may,
of course, be denied of anything else.

When we say "Romulus was the founder of Rome," we
mean that the two terms stand for the same individual.
And such is our meaning also when we affirm, that "this
river is the Thames."

On the other hand, those terms which are called *"Common"* (as opposed to "Singular") from their being capable
of standing for any, or for every, individual of a Class,—
such as "man," "river," country"—may of course be
affirmed of whatever belongs to that Class: as, "the Thames
is a river;" "the Rhine and the Ganges are rivers."

And observe that throughout these Lessons we mean
a "Class" not merely a Head or general description to
which several things are *actually* referred, but one to
which an indefinite number of things *might, conceivably,*
be referred : namely, as many as, (in the colloquial phrase)
may "answer to the *description.*"   For instance, we may
conceive that when the first created man existed alone,
some beings of a Superior Order may have contemplated
him, not merely as a single individual bearing the *proper-
name* "Adam," but also (by Abstraction, which we shall
treat of presently) as possessing those attributes which
we call collectively, *"human nature;"* and they may have
applied to him a name—such as "Man"—implying those
attributes [that *"description"*], and nothing else ; and
which would consequently suit equally well any of his
descendants.

When therefore anything is said to be "referred to such and such a Class," we mean either what *is*, or what *might* be a Class, comprehending any objects that are "of a certain description;" which description (and nothing else) is implied by the "Common-term" which is a name of any, or all, of those objects.

§ 2. A Common-term is thence called (in relation to the "Subjects" to which it is applicable) a "*Predicate;*" that is *affirmatively*-predicable; from its capability of being affirmed of another Term.

A Singular term, on the contrary, may be the *Subject* of a proposition, but not the *Predicate*: unless of a *Negative*-proposition; (as "the first-born of Isaac was not Jacob;") or unless the Subject and Predicate be merely two expressions for the same individual; as in some of the examples above.

You are to remember, however, that a Common-term must be one that can be affirmed of an indefinite number of other terms, *in the same sense*, as applied to each of them : as "vegetable" to "grass," and to an "oak." For different as these are, they are both "vegetables" in the same sense : that is, the word "vegetable" denotes the same thing in respect of both of them: [or, "denotes something *common* to the two."]

But there are several proper-names which are borne, each, by many individuals; such as "John," "William," &c., and which are said to be (in ordinary discourse) very *common* names; that is, very *frequent*. But none of these is what we mean by a "*Common term;*" because, though applied to several persons, it is not in the same sense, but always as denoting, in each case, *one distinct individual.*

If I say, "King Henry was the conqueror at Agincourt," and, "the conqueror of Richard the Third was King Henry," it is not, in sense, *one* term, that occurs in both those propositions. But if I say, of each of these two individuals, that he was a "King," the term "King" is applied to each of them in the same sense.

§ 3. A Common-term, such as "King," is said to have several "*Significates;*" that is, things to which it may be applied : but if it be applied to every one of these *in the same sense*, [or denotes in each of them the same thing] it has but *one* "*signification*." And a Common-term thus applied, is said to be employed "univocally."

If a term be used in several senses, it is, in meaning, not *one* term only, but *several*. Thus, when "Henry" (or any other such name) is applied to two individuals to denote, in each case, *that one distinct person*, it is used not as *one* term, but as *two;* and it is said to be applied to those two, "*equivocally*."

The like often occurs in respect of Common-terms also; that is, it oftens happens that one word or phrase, will be not merely *one*, but *several* Common-terms.

Take for example the word "Case," used to signify a kind of "*covering;*" and again (in Grammar) an inflection of a noun: (as "him" is the accusative [or objective] *case* of "he;") and again a "*case*" such as is laid before a lawyer. The word is, in sense, three; and in each of the three senses may be applied "*univocally*" to several things which are, in that sense, signified by it. But when applied to a *box* and to a *grammatical case*, it is used "equivocally."

§ 4. That process in the mind by which we are enabled to employ Common-terms, is what is called "Generalization;" Common-terms being often called also "*General-terms*."

When in contemplating several objects that *agree* in some point, we "*abstract*" [or *draw off*] and consider separately that point of agreement, disregarding everything wherein they differ, we can then designate them by a *Common-term*, applicable to them, only in respect of that which is "*common*" to them all, and which expresses nothing of the differences between them. And we obtain in this way, either a term denoting the *individuals them-selves* thus agreeing *considered in respect of* that agreement, (which is called a *concrete*-common-term), or, again, a term denoting that *circumstance itself wherein* they agree ; which is called an *abstract*-common-term.

Thus we may contemplate in the mind several different "kings" putting out of our thoughts the name and indivi-dual character of each, and the times and places of their reigns, and considering only the *regal Office* which belongs to all and each of them. And we are thus enabled to designate any or every one of them by the "common" [or general] term, "king:" or again by the term "royalty" we can express the circumstance itself which is common to them.   And so in the case of any other common-term.

The "*Abstraction*" which here takes place, is so called from a Latin-word originally signifying to "draw off;" because we separate, and as it were, draw off, in each of the objects before us, that point—apart from every other —in which they are alike.

It is by doing this, that "Generalization" is effected. But the two words have not the same meaning.   For though we cannot "*generalize*" without "*abstracting*" we may perform Abstraction without Generalization.

§ 5. If, for instance, any one is thinking of "the Sun," without having any notion that there is more than *one* such body in the Universe, he may consider it without any reference to its *place* in the sky ; whether rising or setting or in any other situation; (though it must *be* always actually in *some* situation;) or again, he may be considering its *heat* alone, without thinking of its *light* ; or of its light alone ; or of its apparent *magnitude;* without any reference either to its light or heat.   Now in each of these cases there would be *Abstraction;* though there would be no *Generalization*, as long as he was contemplating only a *single* individual; that which we call the "Sun."

But if he came to the belief (which is that of most Astronomers) that each of the *fixed* Stars is a body affording light and heat of itself, as our Sun does, he might then, by *absracting* this *common* circumstance, apply to all and each of these (the Sun of our System and the Stars) one common-term denoting that circumstance ; calling them all "Suns."   And this would be, to "*generalize*."

In the same manner, a man might, in contemplating a single mountain, (suppose, Snowdon), make its *height* alone, independently of everything else, the subject of his thoughts ; or its *total bulk ;* disregarding its *shape* and the *substances* it is composed of ; or again, its shape alone; and yet while thus abstracting he might be contemplating but the single individual.   But if he abstracted the circumstance *common* to Snowdon, Etna, Lebanon, &c., and denoted it by the common-term "Mountain," he would then be said to generalize. He would then be considering each, not as to its *actual existence as a single individual*, but as to its general character, as being of *such a description* as would apply equally to some other single objects.

§ 6. Any one of these common-terms then serves as a "*Sign*" [or Representative] of a Class; and may be applied. to,—that is, affirmed of—all, or any, of the things it is thus taken to stand for.

And you will have perceived from the above explanations, that what is expressed by a common-term is merely an *inadequate—incomplete notion* [or "view" taken] of *an individual*. For if, in thinking of some individual object, you *retain* in your mind all the circumstances (of character time, place, &c.,) which *distinguish* it (or which might distinguish it) from others,—including the circumstance of *unity* [or singleness]—then any name by which you might denote it, when thus viewed, would be a *Singular*-term; but if you *lay aside* and disregard all these circumstances, and abstract [consider separately] merely the points which are *common*—or which conceivably *might* be common—to it with other individuals, you may then, by taking this incomplete view [or, "apprehension"] of it, apply to it a name expressing nothing that is *peculiar* to it; and which consequently will equally well apply to each of those others; in short, a common-term; such as those in the above examples.

§ 7. You are to remember then, that there is not in the case of these "general" [or common] Terms, (as there is in the case of *Singular*-terms), some real *thing* corresponding to each Term, existing independently of the Term, and of which that term is merely the *name*: in the same manner as "Lebanon" is the name of an actually-existing single individual.

At first sight, indeed, you might imagine that as any "individual man" of your acquaintance, or "Great Britain" or "the Sun," &c., has an existence in nature quite independent of the *name* you call it by, so, in like manner, there must be some *one real thing* existing in nature of which the common-term "Man" or the term "Island" is merely the *name*.

And some writers will tell you that this *thing*, which is the subject of your thoughts when you are employing a general-term, is, the *"abstract-idea"* of Man, of Island, of Mountain, &c. But you will find no one able to explain what sort of a thing any such "abstract idea" can be, which is *one* thing, and yet *not* an *individual*, and which may exist at one and the same time in the minds of *several* different person.*

All the obscure and seemingly-profound disquisitions that you may perhaps meet with, respecting these supposed "abstract-ideas" will but perplex and bewilder you.

Whether the writers of these disquisitions have themselves understood their own meaning, we need not here inquire. But the simple explanation that has been above given of the origin and use of Common-terms, you will be able, with moderate attention, clearly to understand. And you will find it quite sufficient for our present purpose.

§ 8. You will perceive from it, that the subject of our thoughts when we are employing a Common-term, is, the *Term itself*, regarded as a *"Sign;"* namely a Sign denoting a certain *inadequate* notion formed [or, view taken] of an individual which in some point *agrees with* [or "resembles"] some other individuals : the notion being, as has been said, "inadequate" or "incomplete," inasmuch as it omits all *peculiarity* that *distinguishes* the one individual from the others ; so that the same single "Sign" may stand equally well for any of them.

And when several persons are all employing and understanding the same Common-term in the same sense, and are thence said (as some writers express it) to have " one and the same idea" at once in the mind of each, this means merely that they are (thus far) all *thinking alike ;* just as several persons are said to be all " in one and the same *posture"* when they have all of them their limbs *placed*

<hr>

* The question here briefly alluded to, and which could not properly be treated of at large in a short elementary work, is that which was at one time fiercely contested, throughout nearly all Europe, between the two rival sects of Philosophers, the *Realists* and the *Nominalists.*

There are several well-known works in which the student may find it fully discussed.—See WHATELY'S *Elements of Logic,* B. iv. c. 5.

alike; and to be of one and the *same* complexion when their skins are coloured alike. ✖

LESSON VIII.

§ 1. It has been shown, how, by taking an inadequate view of an individual, disregarding every point wherein it differs from certain other individuals, and abstracting that wherein it agrees with them, we can then employ a Common-term as a sign to express all or any of them : and that this process is called "generalization."

It is plain, that the same process may be further and further extended, by continuing to abstract from each of the Classes [or Common-terms] thus formed, the circumstance wherein it agrees with some others, leaving out and disregarding the points of difference ; and thus forming a still *more* general and comprehensive term.

From an individual "Cedar," for instance, you may arrive in this manner at the notion expressed by the Common-term "Cedar," and thence again proceed to the more general term "Tree," and thence again to "Vegetable," &c.

And so, also, you may advance from any "ten" objects before you,) for instance, the fingers ; from which doubtless arose the custom of reckoning by tens,) to the general term,—the number "ten;" and thence again to the more general term, "number;" and ultimately to the term "quantity."

§ 2. The faculty of Abstraction,—at least the ready exercise of it in the employment of Signs [Common-terms], seems to be the chief distinction of the Human Intellect from that of Brutes. These, as is well known, often display much intelligence of another kind, in cases where *Instinct* can have no place: especially in the things which have been *taught* to the more docile among domesticated animals. But the Faculty of *Language*, such as can serve for an *Instrument of Reasoning*,—that is, considered as consisting of arbitrary *general Signs*,— seems to be wanting in Brutes.

They do possess, in a certain degree, the use of Language considered as a *mode of communication;* for it is well known that horses, and dogs, and many other animals understand something of what is said to them; and some brutes can learn to utter sounds indicating certain feelings or perceptions. But they cannot—from their total want, or at least great deficiency, of the power of Abstraction—be taught to use language as an Instrument of Reasoning.

Accordingly, even the most intelligent Brutes seem incapable of forming any distinct notion of *number;* to do which evidently depends on Abstraction. For in order to *count* any objects, you must withdraw your thoughts from all *differences* between them and regard them simply as *units.* And, accordingly, the Savage Tribes (who are less removed than we are from the Brutes) are remarked for a great deficiency in their notions of *number.* Few of them can count beyond ten, or twenty; and some of the rudest Savages have no words to express any numbers beyond five.

And universally, it is in all matters where the exercise of *Abstraction* is concerned, that the inferiority of Savages to Civilized men is the most remarkable.

§ 3. That we do, necessarily, employ Abstraction in order to *reason,* you will perceive from the foregoing explanations and examples. For you will have observed that there can be no Syllogism without a Common-term.

And accordingly, a *Deaf-mute,* before he has been taught a Language,—either the Finger-language, or Reading—cannot carry on a train of Reasoning, any more than a Brute. He differs indeed from a Brute in possessing the mental *capability* of employing Language; but he can no more *make use* of that capability, till he is in possession of some *System of Arbitrary general-signs,* than a person born blind from a Cataract can make use of his capacity of Seeing, till the Cataract is removed.

You will find accordingly, if you question a Deaf-mute who has been taught Language after having grown up, that no such thing as a train of Reasoning had ever passed through his mind before he was taught.

c

If indeed we did reason by means of those "Abstract-ideas," which some persons talk of, and if the Language we used served *merely* to *communicate* with other men, then a person would be able to reason who had no knowledge of any *arbitrary Signs.* But there are no grounds for believing that this is possible; nor, consequently, that "Abstract-ideas" (in that sense of the word) have any existence at all.

You will have observed also, from what has been said, that the Signs [Common-terms] we are speaking of as necessary for the Reasoning-process need not be addressed to the *ear.* The signs of the numbers—the figures 1, 2, 3, 4, &c.,—have no necessary connexion with *sound;* but are equally understood by the English, French, Dutch, &c., whose *spoken*-languages are quite different.

And the *whole* of the *written*-language of the Chinese is of this kind. In the different Provinces of China, they *speak* different Dialects; but all *read* the same characters; each of which (like the figures 1, 2, 3, &c.) has a sense quite independent of the sound.

And to the Deaf-mutes, it must be so with all kinds of Language understood by them; whether Common Writing, or the Finger-language.*

---

* There have been some very interesting accounts published, by travellers in America, and by persons residing there, of a girl named Laura Bridgeman, who has been from birth, not only deaf and dumb, but also blind. She has, however, been taught the finger language, and even to read what is printed in raised characters, and also to write.

The remarkable circumstance in reference to the present subject, is, that when she is alone, her *fingers are generally observed to be moving,* though the signs are so slight and imperfect, that others cannot make out what she is thinking of. But if they inquire of her she will tell them.

It seems that, having once learned the use of *Signs,* she finds the necessity of them as an *Instrument of thought,* when thinking of any thing beyond mere individual objects of sense.

And doubtless every one else does the same; though in *our* case, no one can (as in the case of Laura Bridgeman) *see* the operation; nor, in general can it be *heard;* though some few persons have a habit of occasionally audibly talking to themselves; or, as it is called "thinking aloud." But the Signs we commonly use in silent reflexion are merely mental *conceptions* of uttered words: and these, doubtless, are such, as could be hardly at all understood by another, even if uttered audibly. For we usually think in a kind of *short-hand* (if one may use the expression), like the notes one sometimes takes down on paper to help the memory, which consist of a word or two,—or even a letter,— to suggest a whole sentence; so that such notes would be unintelligible to any one else.

It has been observed also that this girl, when asleep, and doubtless dreaming, has her fingers frequently in motion; being in fact talking in her sleep.

§ 4. By the exercise of Abstraction, (it is to be further remarked,) we not only can separate, and consider apart from the rest, some circumstance belonging to every one of several individuals before the mind, so as to denote them by a general ["common"] term,—and can also by repeating the process, advance to *more and more general* terms ;—but we are also able to fix, arbitrarily, on whatever circumstance we choose to abstract, according to the particular purpose we may have in view.

Suppose, for instance, it is some individual "Building" that we are considering : in respect of its *materials* we may refer it to the class (suppose) of "Stone-buildings," or of "wooden," &c.; in respect of its *use*, it may be (suppose) a "house," as distinguished from a Chapel, a Barn, &c.; in respect of Orders of *Architecture*, it may be a "Gothic building," or a "Grecian," &c.; in respect of *size*, it may be a "large," or a "small building;" in respect of *color*, it may be "white," "red," "brown," &c.

And so with respect to anything else that may be the subject of our reasoning, on each occasion that occurs. We arbitrarily fix on, and abstract, out of all the things actually existing in the subject, that one which is important to the purpose in hand.   So that the same thing is referred to one Class or to another, (of all those to which it really *is* referable,) according to the occasion.

For instance, in the example above, you might refer the "building" you were speaking of, to the Class [or Predicable] of "*white*-buildings,"—or even of "*white-objects*,"—if your purpose were to show that it might be used as a *land-mark;* if you were reasoning concerning its danger from *fire*, you might class it (supposing it were of *wood*) not only with such *buildings*, but also with hay-stacks and other combustibles: if the building were about to be *sold*, along with, perhaps, not only other buildings, but likewise cattle, land, farming implements, &c., that were for sale at the same time, the point you would then abstract, would be, its being *an article of value*.   And so in other cases.

§ 5. You must perceive clearly, that we are not to consider each object as *really* and properly *belonging to* and forming a portion of, some *one* Class only, rather than any other that may with truth be affirmed of it; and that it depends on the *particular train of thought* we happen to be engaged in, *what* it is that is important and proper to be noticed, and what again, is an insignificant circumstance, and foreign from the question.

But some persons who have been always engaged in some one pursuit or occupation, without attending to any other, are apt to acquire a narrow-minded habit of regarding almost everything in one particular point of view; that is, considering each object in reference only to their own pursuit.

For instance, a mere Botanist might think it something strange and improper, if he heard an agriculturist classing together, under the title of "artificial *grasses*," such plants as Clover, Tares, and Rye-grass; which botanically are widely different. And the mere farmer might no less think it strange to hear the troublesome "weed" (as he has been used to call it) that is known by the name of "Couch-grass," ranked by the Botanist as a species of "wheat," the "Triticum repens," the farmer having been accustomed to rank it along with "nettles, and thistles;" with which it has no *botanical* connexion.

Yet neither of these classifications [or "generalizations"] would be in itself erroneous and improper: though it would be improper, in a Work on *Natural History* to class plants according to their *agricultural uses;* or, in an agricultural Treatise, to consider principally (as the Botanist does) the structure of their *flowers*.

So also, it would be quite impertinent to take into consideration a man's learning or ability, if the question were as to the allowance of food requisite for his support; or his stature, if you were inquiring into his qualifications as a statesman; or the amount of his property, if you were inquiring into his state of health; or his muscular strength, if the question were as to his moral character: though each of these might be important in reference to a different inquiry.

The great importance of attending to these points, you will easly perceive, by referring to the analysis of Reasoning which has been above given. For as the proving of any Conclusion consists in *referring* that of which something is to be affirmed or denied, to a class [or Predicable] of which that affirmation or denial can be made, our ability in Reasoning must depend on our power of *abstracting* correctly, clearly, and promptly from the subject in question, that which may furnish a "middle-term" suitable to the occasion.

PART II.

COMPENDIUM.

LESSON IX.

§ 1. We have gone through, in the way of a slight sketch, the *Analysis* of Reasoning. To analyse (as has been already explained) means to "take to pieces" so as to resolve anything into its *elements* [or component-parts.] Thus a Chemist is said to "analyse" any compound substance that is before him, when he exhibits separately the simpler substances it is composed of, and resolves these again into their elements. And when, again, he *combines* these elements into their compounds, and those again into furthur compounds—thus reversing the former process, (which is called the "analytical,") he is said to be proceeding *synthetically :* the word "Synthesis"—which signifies "putting together," — being the opposite of "Analysis."

Accordingly, it has been shown, in the foregoing Lessons, that every train of Argument being capable of being exhibited in a series of Syllogisms, a Syllogism contains three Propositions, and a Proposition two Terms. And it has been shown, how "Common-terms" (which are indispensable for reasoning) are obtained by means of Abstraction from Individual objects.

This analytical method is the best suited for the *first introduction* of any study to a learner; because he there sees, from the very beginning, the practical application of whatever is taught. But the opposite method—the synthetical—is the more convenient for *storing up* in the mind all that is to be remembered.

We shall therefore now go over a great part of the same ground in a reversed order, merely *referring* to such things as have been already taught, and adding such further rules, and explanation of additional technical-terms, as may be needed.

§ 2. The act of the mind in taking in the meaning of a Term, is called, in technical language, the act [or "operation"] of "Simple apprehension;" that is, "*mere* apprehension," [or "apprehension only."]   When a proposition is stated—which consists, as we have seen, of two terms, one of which is affirmed or denied of the other —the "operation" [or "act"] of the mind is technically called "Judgment." And the two terms are described in technical language, as "compared" together, and as "agreeing," or as "disagreeing," according as you *affirm* or *deny*, the one of the other.

When from certain Judgments you proceed to another Judgment resulting from them,—that is, when you *infer* [or deduce] a Proposition from certain other Propositions —this "operation" is called "Reasoning" or "Argumentation," or (in the language of some writers) "Discourse."

And these are all the mental operations that we are at present concerned with.

Each of these operations is liable to a corresponding defect; namely, "Simple-apprehension" to *indistinctness*, "Judgment" to *falsity*, and "Reasoning" to *inconclusiveness;* [or fallaciousness.] And it is desirable to avail ourselves of any rules and cautions as to the employment of language, that may serve to guard against these defects, to the utmost degree that is possible: in other words, to guard, by the best rules we can frame, against *Terms* not conveying a distinct meaning;—against *false Propositions* mistaken for true,—and against *apparent-arguments* [or "Fallacies" or "Sophisms"] which are in reality *inconclusive*, though likely to be mistaken for real [valid] arguments.

And such a system of Rules,* based on a scientific view of the Reasoning-process, and of everything connected with it, is what the ancient Greeks, among whom it originated, called the "Dialectic-art;" from a word signifying to "discourse on," or "discuss" a subject.

§ 3. You are to observe, however, two important distinctions in reference to the above-mentioned defects;

---

* You are to observe, that a Science properly consists of *general truths* that are to be known: an Art, of *practical rules* for something that is to be *done*.

1st, you are to remember that which *is*, *really*, a Term, may be *indistinctly* apprehended by the person employing it, or by his hearer; and so also, a Proposition which is *false*, is not the less a *real Proposition ;* but, on the other hand, any expression or statement which does not really *prove* anything is *not, really*, an argument at all, though it may be brought forward and passed off as such.

2ndly, it is to be remembered, that (as it is evident from what has been just said) no rules can be devised that will *equally* guard against *all three* of the above-mentioned defects.

To arrive at a distinct apprehension of everything that may be expressed by any term whatever, and again, to ascertain the truth or falsity of every conceivable Proposition, is manifestly beyond the reach of any system of rules. But, on the other hand, it *is* possible to exhibit any pretended Argument whatever in such a form as to be able to *pronounce decisively* on it validity or its fallaciousness.

So that the *last* of three defects alluded to (though not the two former) may be *directly* and *completely* obviated by the application of suitable rules. But the other two defects can be guarded against, (as will presently be shown,) only *indirectly*, and to a certain degree.

In other words, rules may be framed that will enable us to decide what is, or is not, *really* a "Term,"—really, a "Proposition,"—or really an "Argument :" and to do this, is to guard *completely* against the defect of *inconclusiveness ;* since nothing that is inconclusive is, really, an "Argument;" though that may be *really* a "Term" of which you do not *distinctly* apprehend the meaning; and that which is *really* a "*Proposition*" may be a *false* Proposition.

§ 4. When two terms are brought together (or "compared," as some express it) as Subject and Predicate of a Proposition, they are (as was above remarked) described in technical language, as "agreeing," or "disagreeing," according as the one is *affirmed* or *denied*, of the other.

This "agreement," however, does not (you are to observe) mean *coincidence;* [or that the two terms are

" equivalent;"] for when I say "Every X is Y," or "Every Sheep is a ruminant-animal," this does not mean "X is *equivalent* to Y;" [or "X" and "Y" are terms of *equal extent;*] indeed, we know that "ruminant-animal" is in fact a term of greater extent than "sheep;" including several other species besides. We only mean to assert that it is a Class [or Predicable] *comprehending under it,* at least the term "Sheep;" but whether it does or does not comprehend anything else besides, the proposition before us *does not declare.*

Hence it is that (as was formerly explained) the Predicate of an *Affirmative*-proposition is considered as *undistributed :* the Subject being compared with *part at least* of the Predicate, and asserted to "agree" with it; but whether there be, or be not, any other part of the Predicate which does *not* agree with that subject, is not *declared* in the proposition itself.

There are, it is to be observed, two *apparent* exceptions to this rule : 1st, the case of a Proposition which gives a *Definition* of anything: as when I say "a triangle is a three-sided figure;" which would not be a correct *definition;* unless it were also true that "every three-sided figure is a triangle ;" and 2ndly, by the case of an affirmative-Proposition, where both terms are *singular*, and denote, of course, one and the same Individual; as "Ishmael was the first-born of Abraham."

In both these cases, the Subject and Predicate are, in each proposition, what are called "convertible" [or "equivalent"] terms. But then, to assert or imply both that a certain affirmative-proposition is *true* and *also* that its terms are *equivalent*, is to make (as was formerly remarked) not merely *one*, but *two* assertions.

Now if I am understood to mean not only that it is true that "a triangle is a three-sided figure," but also that *this is the definition* of a "triangle," then, I am understood as making two assertions; that not only "every triangle is a three-sided figure," but also that "every three-sided figure is a triangle." But this is understood not from the *Proposition* itself, looking to the *form of expression alone*, but from what we know, or think, respecting the *sense of the Terms* themselves, or from what we suppose the speaker to have intended by those Terms. For, all that is implied in the *mere form* of an affirmative-proposition,—as "X is Y"—is simply that *some part at least* of the term "Y" (whatever that symbol may stand for), is pronounced to agree with the term "X."

§ 5. And a like explanation will apply in the other case also. If I understand from the *sense of the terms* in some affirmative-proposition, that the Subject and the Predicate are each a Singular-term (denoting, of course, one and the same individual), as "Ishmael was the first-born of Abraham," then I understand, as implied by the *meaning of the words* (though not, by the *form* of the *Proposition*) *another* proposition also ; namely, that " the first-born of Abraham was Ishmael." In short, it is from my knowledge of the sense of the terms themselves that I understand them to be "convertible" [or equivalent] terms. For you may observe, that a Singular-term must. from its own nature, correspond to a *Common-term taken universally*, [or "distributed"], inasmuch as it *cannot but* stand for the *whole* (not merely some part) of that which it denotes.

In such cases as the above, then, that which is *expressed as one* proposition, is so understood from the meaning of the words as in reality to *imply two*. And there is, therefore, no real exception to the rule, that an Affirmative-proposition does not, *by the form of the expression*, distribute its Predicate.

§ 6. That which pronounces the *agreement* or *disagreement* of the two Terms of a Proposition [or which makes it *affirmative* or *negative*] is called, as has been above said, the "Copula." And this is always in sense, either "is" or "is not." For every *Verb*, except what is called the "Substantive-verb" to "be," contains something more than a bare assertion of the agreement or disagreement of two terms. It always contains in it the Predicate (or part of the Predicate) also.

Thus, the proposition "it rains" (which in Latin would be expressed by the single word "pluit") is resolved
Sub.   Cop.   Pred.
into "Rain—is—falling;" or in some such way. "John
Subj.   Cop.
owes William a pound," is resolved into "John—is—

Pred.
owing [or indebted to] William a Pound." And so in all such cases.

Sometimes, indeed, even the substantive-verb itself is both Copula and Predicate; namely, where *existence* alone is affirmed or denied; as "God is;" "one of Jacob's sons is not";* in which cases "existing" is the Predicate.

You are to observe, that the Copula has in itself no relation to *time*. If, therefore, any other *tense* besides the *Present*, of the Substantive-verb, is used, it is to be understood as the same in sense with the *Present*, as far as the *assertion* is concerned; the difference of tense being regarded (as well as the *person* and *number*) merely as a matter of grammatical propriety: unless it be where the circumstance of *time* really does affect the sense of the proposition. And then this circumstance is to be regarded as part of one of the *Terms;* as, "this man *was* honest;" that is, "he is one *formerly-honest*." In such a case, an emphasis, with a peculiar tone, is laid on the word "*was*."

An *infinitive*, you are to observe, is not a Verb (since it can contain no affirmation or denial), but a verbal noun-substantive. And a *Participle*, again, is a verbal adjective.

A Participle, or any other Adjective, may be made a *Predicate*, but not (by itself) a subject of a proposition; as "this grass is green," "that grass is mown."

An infinitive, though generally placed (in English) at the *end* of a sentence, is almost always (when it is by itself a Term) the *Subject;* as "I like to ride;" that is,

Sub.   Pred.
"To ride, [or "riding"] is—a thing I like."

And observe that there is, in English, an infinitive in "*ing*," the same in sound with the Participle, but different in sense. When I say "Riding" [or "to ride"] "is pleasant," and again "that man is riding," in the former sentence the word "riding" is a Substantive, and is the Subject; in the latter it is an adjective [Participle] and is the Predicate.

---

* Gen. xlii. 13.

One infinitive, however, is sometimes predicated of *another* infinitive: as, "seeing is believing;" "not to advance is to fall back;" "to be born is not to be perfected."

§ 7. A term may consist (as was formerly explained) of one word, or of several. And care must be taken, when you are examining a proposition, not to mistake for one of its Terms a word which, though it might have been used as a Term, is, in *that proposition*, only a part of a Term. Thus, in one of the above examples, the word "pound" is not one of the Terms, but only a part of the Term "owing a pound to William." A *description* of some object will sometimes occupy a page or two, and yet be only the Predicate of a single Proposition.

You are to observe, also, that one single sentence will often imply what may be regarded as several distinct Propositions; each, indeed, implying the *truth* of the others, but having their terms different, according as we understand the *drift* (as it is called) or design of what is uttered: that is, according to what we understand the person to be speaking of (which is the subject), and what it is that he says [predicates] of it.

Thus "He—did not—design—your—death"—may be regarded as any one of at least four different propositions. If (No. 1.), the word "He" be marked by emphasis in speaking, or by italics, it will be understood as the Predicate; and the drift of the sentence will be, that "whoever else may have designed your death, it was not *He*:" if the emphasis fall on No. 2, the Predicate will be "designing," [or by "design"], and the drift of the sentence will be, that "though he may have endangered your life, it was not by *design*:" and so with the rest.

You should endeavour, therefore, so to express yourself, as to make it clearly understood not only what is the meaning of *each word* you employ, but also what is the general *drift of the whole* sentence; in short, what is the Subject of your Proposition, and what it is that you say of it. And as far as you can, you should make this clear by the *structure* of each sentence, without resorting to the expedient of *italics* or under-scoring oftener than is unavoidable.

There is frequently a great advantage towards such clearness, gained by the English word "IT" in that sense in which it stands (not as the *neuter* pronoun, answering to "He" and "She," but) as the *representative of the Subject* of a Proposition, of whatever Gender or number; so as to allow the subject itself to be placed last: as—

Subj.   Cop.   Pred.   Subj.

" It—is not—he — that had this design:"

Or again—

Subj.   Cop.   Pred.   Subj.

" It—is not — by design—that he did this," &c.

LESSON X.

§ 1. A Proposition is, as has been said, an act of judgment expressed in words; and is defined to be a "Sentence which *asserts;*" or, in the language of some writers, an "indicative Sentence:" "*indicative,*" [or "asserting,"] meaning "that which *affirms* or *denies* something." It is this that distinguishes a *Proposition* from a *Question*, or a *Command*, &c.

Propositions considered merely as *Sentences*, are distinguished into "Categorical" and " Hypothetical."

The Categorical asserts simply, that the Predicate does, or does not, apply to the Subject: as "the world had an intelligent Maker:" "Man is not capable of raising himself, unassisted, from the savage to the civilized state." The Hypothetical [called by some writers, "Compound"] makes its assertion under a *Condition*, or with an *Alternative;* as "if the World is not the work of chance, it must have had an intelligent Maker:" "Either mankind are capable of rising into civilization unassisted, or the first beginning of civilization must have come from above."

The former of these two last examples is of that kind called "Conditional-proposition;"* the "*condition*" being denoted by "if," or some such word. The latter example is of the kind called "Disjunctive;" the *alternative* being denoted by "either " and "or."

---

* Or, "hypothetical" according to those writers who use the word "compound" when we have used "hypothetical."

The division of Propositions into Categorical and Hypothetical, is, as has been said, a division of them considered merely as *Sentences;* for a light distinction might be extended to other kinds of Sentences also. Thus "Are men capable of raising themselves to civilization?" "Go and study books of travels," are what might be called *categorical sentences*, though not *propositions.* "If man is incapable of civilizing himself, whence came the first beginning of civilization?" might be considered as a *conditional question;* and "Either admit the conclusion, or refute the argument," is a *disjunctive command.*

At present we shall treat only of Categorical Propositions.

§ 2. It has been above explained, that Propositions (of this Class,—the Categorical) are divided according to their "Quantity" into "Universal" and "Particular;"— that an "*Indefinte*-proposition" is in reality either the one or the other; though the form of expression does not declare *which* is meant:—and also that a "*Singular*-proposition is equivalent to "Universal," since its subject cannot but stand for the whole of what that Term denotes, when that whole is one single individual.

You have also learnt that propositions are divided, according to their "Quality," into "affirmative" and "negative." The division of them, again, into "true" and "false" is also called a division according to their "quality;" namely, the "quality of *Matter;*" (as it has relation to the subject-matter one is treating of;) while the other kind of quality (a proposition's being *affirmative* or *negative*) is "the quality of the *expression.*"

The "quality of the matter" is considered (in relation to our present inquiries) as *accidental*, and the "quality of the expression" as *essential.* For though the truth or falsity of a proposition—for instance, in Natural-history, is the most essential point *in reference to Natural-history,* and of a *mathematical* proposition in reference to *Mathematics*, and so in other cases,—this is merely accidental in reference to an inquiry (such as the present) only as to *forms of expression.* In reference to *that*, the essential difference is that between affirmation and negation.

And here it should be remarked by the way, that as

on the one hand, every *Proposition* must be either true or false, so, on the other hand, *nothing else* can be, strictly speaking, either true or false. In colloquial language, however, "true" and "false" are often more loosely applied; as when men speak of the "*true* cause" of anything; meaning "the *real* cause;"—the "true heir," that is, the *rightful* heir;—a "*false* prophet,"—that is, a *pretended* prophet, or one who *utters falsehoods;*—a "true" or "false" argument, meaning a *valid* [real], or an *apparent*-argument—a man "true" or "false" to his friend; *i. e., faithful*, or unfaithful, &c.

A Proposition, you are to observe, is Affirmative or Negative, according to its *Copula*; *i. e.*, according as the Predicate is affirmed or denied of the Subject. Thus, "not to advance, is to fall back," is *affirmative;* "No miser is truly rich" [or "a miser is not truly rich"] is a *negative.* "*A few* of the sailors were saved," is an affirmative; "*Few* of the sailors were saved," is properly a negative: for it would be understood that you were speaking of "most of the sailors" and *denying* that they were saved.

Since then every Proposition must be either Affirmative or Negative, and also, either Universal or Particular, Propositions are considered as divided (taking into account both Quantity *and* Quality) into four Classes; which, for brevity's sake, are usually denoted by the Symbols A, E, I, O; namely A, Universal-affirmative, E, Universal-negative, I, Particular-affirmative, and O, Particular-negative.

§ 3. Any two Propositions are, technically, said to be "*opposed*" to each other, when, "having the same Subject and Predicate, they differ either in Quantity or in Quality, or in both."

In ordinary language, however, (and in some technical treatises) propositions are not to be reckoned as "opposed" unless they differ in *Quality*.

It is evident that with any given Subject and Predicate, you may state four distinct Propositions, A, E, I, and O; any two of which are said to be "opposed." And hence there are (in the language of most technical writers) reckoned four kinds of "Opposition." 1st, A and E,—

the two Universals, Affirmative and Negative, (always supposing the *Terms* the same) are called "*Contraries*" to each other: 2nd, The Two Particulars, I and O, "*Subcontraries.*" 3rd, The Two Affirmatives again, or the two Negatives, (A and I, or again, E and O,) are called "*Subalterns;*" and 4th, those which differ both in Quantity and Quality—as A and O, or E and I,—are called *Contradictories.*"

It is usual to exhibit in a Scheme (such as that below) these four kinds of "Opposition;" by placing at the corners of a Square the Symbols A, E, I, O, as representing, respectively, the above-mentioned four classes of Propositions.

n. *t.*   A – – – – Contraries – – – – E   n. *f.*
i. *f.*   [Every X is Y.]   [No X is Y.]   i. *t.*
c. *f.*   c. *f.*

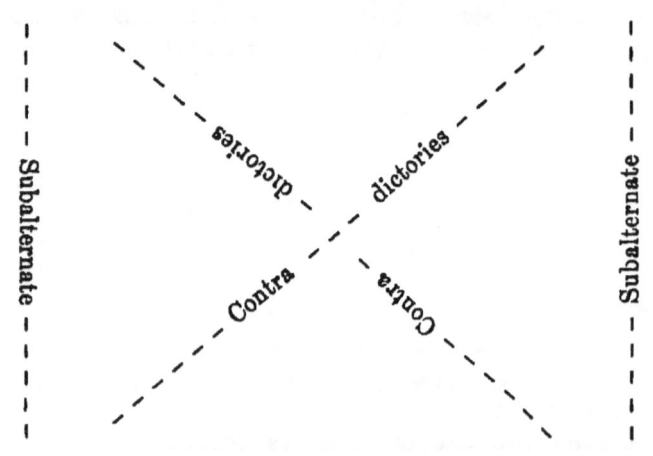

n. *t.*   I – – – – Subcontraries – – – – O   n. *f.*
i. *f.*   [Some X is Y.]   [Some X is not Y.]   i. *t.*
c. *t.*   c. *t.*

You may substitute for the unmeaning Symbols, X, Y, (which stand for the Terms of the above Propositions) whatever significant Terms you will; and on their meaning, of course, will depend the truth or falsity of each Proposition.

For instance, Naturalists have observed, that "animals having horns on the head are universally ruminant;" that, of "carnivorous animals" none are ruminant; and that of "animals with hoofs," some are ruminant, and some not. Let us take then instead of "X," "animals with horns on the head," and for "Y," "ruminant:" here, the real connection of the Terms in respect of their meaning— which connection is called the *"matter"* of a proposition— is such that the Predicate may be affirmed universally of the subject; and of course the *affirmatives* (whether Universal or Particular) will be true, and the "negatives" false. In this case, the "matter" is technically called "necessary," inasmuch as we *cannot avoid believing* the Predicate to be applicable to the Subject.

Again let "X" represent "carnivorous animal," and "Y" "ruminant;" this is a case of what is called "impossible matter;" (*i.e.* where we *cannot believe it possible for* the Predicate to be applicable to the Subject) being just the reverse of the foregoing; and, of course, both the Affirmatives will here be false, and both negatives true.

And lastly, as an instance of what is called "contingent matter," *i.e.* where the Predicate can neither be affirmed universally, nor denied universally, of the Subject, take "hoofed animal" for "X" and "ruminant" for "Y;" and of course the universals will both be false, and the Particulars, true: that is, it is equally true, that "some hoofed animals are ruminant," and that "some are not."

§ 4. You will perceive then, on examining such a Scheme, that *"contrary"* Propositions can never be both of them true, though they may (viz.: in "contingent-matter") be both false: that "*Sub*-contraries," on the other hand, may be both true, but never both false: that "*Contradictories*" [*diametrically*-opposite Propositions] must in in every case be, one true, and the other false: and that *"Subalterns"* (of which the Universal is called the "Subaltern*ant*," and the Particular "Subaltern*ate*") may be either both true, or both false, or the one true and the other false.

These last propositions, however, though reckoned, as has been said above, by most dialectical writers, among those *opposed*, are not so accounted in ordinary discourse.

The four kinds of Propositions, A, E, I, O, have been in the Scheme, marked, each, with the letters *t* for "true" and *f* for "false," and also with the letters *n, i, c,* to denote the three kinds of matter, (necessary, impossible, contingent), in order to point out *which* propositions are true, and which false, in each kind of matter.

The technical terms we have here explained, arc needful to be learnt, as being some of them in frequent use, and as being convenient for the avoiding of circumlocution and of indistinctness.

"Contradictory-opposition" is the kind most frequently alluded to, because (as is evident from what has been just said) to *deny,*—or to *disbelieve*—a proposition, is to *assert* or to *believe,* its Contradictory; and of course, to *assent to,* or *maintain* a proposition, is to reject its Contradictory. Belief, therefore, and Disbelief are not *two different* states of the mind, but the *same,* only considered in reference to two Contradictory propositions. And consequently *Credulity* and *Incredulity* are not opposite habits, but the same; in reference to some class of propositions, and to their contradictories.*

For instance, he who is the most *incredulous* respecting a certain person's *guilt,* is, in other words, the most ready to believe him *not guilty;* he who is the most credulous† as to certain works being within the reach of Magic is the most incredulous [or "slow of heart to believe"] that they are *not* within the reach of Magic; and so in all cases.

The reverse of *believing this* or *that individual* proposition, is, no doubt, to *disbelieve that same* proposition: but the reverse of *belief generally,* is (not disbelief; since that implies belief; but) *doubt.*

And there may even be cases in which *doubt* itself may amount to the most extravagant credulity. For instance, if any one should "doubt whether there is any such Country as Egypt," he would be in fact *believing* this most incredible proposition; that "it is *possible* for many thousands of persons, unconnected with each other, to have agreed, for successive Ages, in bearing witness to

---

* The word *"credulity"* is sometimes understood as limited to the sense of overhasty belief in *testimony.* But there seems no objection to its being employed, generally, to signify "hasty belief, on insufficient grounds, of whatever kind." To all practical purposes, at least, this may be regarded as credulity.

† As the Jews, in the time of Jesus, in respect of his works.

the existence of a fictitious Country, without being de-
tected, contradicted, or suspected."

All this, though self-evident, is, in practice, frequently
lost sight of.

§ 5. A Proposition is said to be "*converted,*" when its
" Terms are transposed;" *i. e.*, when the Subject is made
the Predicate, and the Predicate the Subject. And when
no other change is made, this is called "simple-conversion."
When, for instance, I say, "no carnivorous animal" is a
"ruminant," the "simple-*converse*" of this would be, "no
ruminant is a carnivorous animal."

The "conversion" of such a proposition as this, "No
one [is happy who] is anxious for a change," would be
effected by altering the arrangement of the words in
brackets, into "who is happy."

The Conversion of a Proposition is said to be "*illative,*"
when the truth of the "*Converse*" is implied (looking
merely to the *form of expression*) "by the truth of the
original proposition;" [or "*exposita;*"] which is the case
in the example above: it being evident that if the former
of those Propositions (whatever may be the meaning of
the Terms) be true, the Converse must be true also. For
to say that "No X is Y," is to imply that "no Y is X."

You are to observe, however, that the Converse of a
true Proposition may happen to be true also, without
the Conversion's being "illative;" that is, when the truth
of that Converse is not implied by the truth of the "Exposita" [the original proposition]. Thus, "Every X is
Y" does not imply that "every Y is X," though it may
happen that both propositions may be true.

For instance, that "Every tree is a vegetable," does not
imply that "every vegetable is a tree;" and this last happens in fact to be not true. But no more is it implied,
when I say, "every equilateral triangle is equiangular,"
that "every equiangular triangle is equilateral:" for though
both these propositions *are* true, the one of them does
not imply the other; and they are separately demonstrated
as distinct propositions, in geometrical treatises.

In order to understand why the simple-conversion of
"every X is Y," into "every Y is X," is not "illative,"
you have only to observe, that, in the "Exposita,"

[original proposition,] "Y" is *undistributed*, as being the predicate of an Affirmative; while, in the "Converse," it is "distributed," by being made the *Subject of a Universal*. A *new Term* is therefore, in fact, introduced; since instead of *part* of the Term "Y" we have employed the *whole* of it; and the agreement or disagreement of one Term with *some part* of another Term, does not imply its agreement or disagreement with *every part* of it; that is, with the whole. For though a part is implied by a whole, a whole is not implied by a part.

When for instance, I say, "every tree is a vegetable," I am employing (as was formerly explained) the term "vegetable" to stand only for *part* of its "significates;" and this does not authorize me to employ it (in the Converse) as standing for *all* its Significates; as in saying that "*every* vegetable is a tree."

And strictly speaking, *that* is not a real "conversion," —but only an "*apparent*-conversion"—which is not "illative." For, (as has been above said,) there is not a *mere transposition* of the terms, but a *new term* introduced, when a term which was undistributed in the "Exposita," is distributed [taken universally] in the Converse.

But as it is usual, in common discourse, to speak of "an *unsound* argument," meaning "an *apparent*-argument, which is in reality *not* an argument," so, in this case also, it is common to say, for instance, that "Euclid proves first that all equilateral triangles are equiangular, and afterwards he proves the *Converse*, that all equiangular triangles are equilateral:" or again, to say, "It is true that all money is wealth;" but I deny the *Converse* (in reality, the *apparent*-converse) that all wealth is money.

§ 6 Conversion then, strictly so called,—that is, "illative-conversion,"—can only take place when no term is distributed in the Converse, which was undistributed in the "Exposita."

Hence, since E [Universal-negative] distributes both terms, and I [a Particular-affirmative] neither, these may both be simply-converted illatively. As in the example above, "no carnivorous animal is ruminant," implies by the very form of the expression, "that no ruminant is a carnivorous animal." And so also, "some things which are strange are believed," implies that, "some things which are believed are strange."

We may also illatively-convert A [a Universal-affirmative] by altering its "*Quantity*" fiom Universal to Particular. For every " X is Y" does not imply that "*some* Y" (though not that "*every* Y") "is X." So, in the example above, we might allowably have stated (though not that "all vegetables," yet) that "some vegetables are trees."

This procedure is called "conversion by *limitation;*" or according to some writers, "conversion per accidens." And it may be applied to E also; as for instance in the example above, you might have said "*Some* ruminant is not carnivorous;" though this would have been to come short of what you were warranted in stating.

But in O [particular-negative] the conversion will not be illative, on account of the rule that the Predicate of a Negative is always distributed. The proposition therefore " Some X is not Y" does not imply that " some Y is not X;" since X is distributed in the "Converse" and was not in the "Exposita," in which it was the Subject of a Particular. It is true that "some men are not negroes:" but this does not imply that "some negroes are not men."

A particular-negative [O] cannot be converted illatively except by changing its *Quality* from negative to affirmative (without altering the sense), by regarding the negation as attached to the PREDICATE instead of to the *Copula.*

$$S \qquad\qquad Cop \qquad\qquad Pr$$
Thus.   " Some X——*is* not——Y," may be taken as an
$$S \qquad\qquad Cop. \qquad\qquad Pr.$$
affirmative, namely, "Some X——is——not Y;" and this latter proposition [I] may of course be simply-converted
$$S \qquad\qquad Cop. \qquad Pr.$$
illatively; as "Some not Y——is——X."

Thus, "Some men are not-negroes," implies that "Some who are not negroes are men;" or (as such a proposition is often expressed) "one may be a man *without* being a negro." So again "Some who possess wealth are not happy," implies that "Some who are not-happy possess wealth.

§ 7. This procedure is technically called " Conversion-by-*negation,*" [or, by " Contraposition"]. It is applicable also to [A] Universal-affirmatives. For, to *affirm* some Predicable of a Subject, or [to assert the *presence* of some attribute] is the same thing in sense as to *deny* its *absence*. Hence a Universal-affirmative may be stated as a Universal-*negative;* which (as we have seen) may be simply-converted.

Thus "Every X is Y" is *equipollent* [or *equivalent* in sense] to "No X is not Y;" which may be illatively converted into "nothing that is not Y—is—X:" [or "whatever is not Y——is not—X"].

So the proposition, "Every true poet is a man of genius," may be stated as "No true poet is—not-a-man-of-genius;" which (being E) may be illatively converted into "no one who is not a man of genius is a true poet:" (as such a proposition is very commonly expressed) "*None but* a man of genius can be a true poet;" or again, "a man of genius *alone* can be a true poet;" or again, "One cannot be a true poet *without* being a man of genuis."

And here it is worth remarking by the way, that in such examples as the above, the words "may," "can," "cannot," &c., have no reference (as they sometimes have) to *power*, as exercised by an agent; but merely to the *distribution* or *non-distribution of Terms;* or to the *confidence* or *doubtfulness* we feel respecting some supposition.

To say, for instance, that "a man who has the plague *may* recover, does not mean that "it is in his *power* to recover if he chooses;" but it is only a form of stating a *particular proposition*: [I] namely, that "*Some* who have the plague recover." And again, to say "there *may* be a bed of coal in this district," means merely, "The existence of a bed of coal in this district—is—a thing which I cannot confidently deny or affirm."

§ 8. So also to say "a virtuous man *cannot* betray his Country" [or "it is *impossible* that a virtuous man should betray," &c.] does not mean that he lacks the *power*, (for there is no *virtue* in not doing what is out of one's power,) but merely that "not betraying one's country" forms an *essential part of the notion* conveyed by the *term* "virtuous." We mean, in short, that it is as much out of *our* power to *conceive* a virtuous man who should be a traitor, **as** to conceive "a Square with *unequal sides;*" that is, a square which is *not* a square. The expression therefore is merely a way of stating the Universal-proposition [E], " No virtuous man betrays his Country."

So again, to say "A weary traveller in the deserts of Arabia *must* eagerly drink when he comes to a Spring," does not mean that *he* is *compelled* to drink, but that *I* cannot *avoid believing* that he will;—that there is no *doubt* in my mind.

In these and many other such instances, the words "may," "must," "can," "impossible," &c., have reference, not to *power* or *absence of power in an agent*, but only to *universality* or absence of Universality in the *expression;* or, to *doubt* or *absence of doubt* in our own mind, respecting what is asserted.

LESSON XI.

§ 1. An Argument [or Act of Reasoning expressed in words] is defined " an Expression in which, from something laid down [assumed as true] something else is concluded to be true, as following necessarily [resulting] from the other." That which follows from the other, is called (as was formerly explained) the *"Conclusion ;"* and that from which it follows, the "Premises;" or in the language of some writers, the "Antecedent."

The above is the strict technical definition. But in ordinary language the word "Argument" is often employed to denote the *Premises* alone ; or, sometimes that one of the Premises which is *expressed*, when the other is *understood :* as when one speaks of proving so and so *by* this or that *argument;* meaning, by such and such a Premise.

And you may observe, by the way, that of the two Premises, the *Major* (formerly explained), is in common discourse often called the " Principle," and the minor-premise the " Reason."

Frequently also in common discourse "an Argument" is used to signify a " Series of arguments," leading ultimately to the Conclusion maintained.

An Argument, if stated in such a regular form that "its conclusiveness [its being really an Argument] is apparent from the mere *form of expression alone,*" (independently of the meaning of the words,) is then called a "Syllogism." As, "Every X is Y ;* Z is X, and therefore Z is Y ;" in which, as was formerly explained, the truth of the Conclusion, assuming the Premises to be true,—must be admitted, whatever terms you may make X, Y, and Z, respectively, stand for.

You are to remember, therefore, that a Syllogism is not (as some have imagined) a *peculiar kind* of Argument; but only a certain *form* in which *every* Argument may be exhibited.

§ 2. One circumstance which has tended to mislead persons as to this point, is, that in a Syllogism we see the conclusion following *certainly* [or *necessarily*] from the Premises; and again, in any apparent-syllogism which on examination is found to be (as you have seen in some of the examples) not a *real* one [not "valid"] the Conclusion *does not follow at all;* and the whole is a mere deception. And yet we often hear of Arguments which have *some* weight, and yet are not quite *decisive ;*—of Conclusions which are rendered *probable*, but not absolutely *certain*, &c. And hence some are apt to imagine that the *conclusiveness* of an Argument admits of *degrees ;* and that sometimes a conclusion may, *probably and partially,*—though not *certainly and completely*—follow from its Premises.

This mistake arises from men's forgetting that the *Premises themselves* will very often be *doubtful ;* and, then, the Conclusion also will be doubtful.

As was shown formerly, one or both of the Premises of a perfectly valid Syllogism may be utterly false and absurd : and then, the Conclusion, though inevitably following from them, may be either true or false, we cannot tell which. And if one or both of the Premises be merely probable, we can infer from them only a *probable* conclusion ; though the *conclusiveness,*—that is, the connection between the Premises and the Conclusion—is perfectly certain.

---

* See above. Lesson IX. § 4.

For instance, assuming that "every month has 30 days" (which is palpably false) then, from the minor-premise that "April is a month," it follows (which happens to be true) that "April has 30 days:" and from the minor-premise that "February is a month," it follows that "February has 30 days;" which is false. In each case the conclusiveness of the Argument is the same; but in every case, when we have ascertained the falsity of one of the Premises, we know nothing (as far as *that argument* is concerned) of the truth or falsity of the Conclusion.

§ 3. When, however, we are satisfied of the falsity of some *Conclusion*, we may, of course, be sure that (at least) one of the Premises is false; since if they had both been true, the Conclusion would have been true.

And this—which is called the "*indirect*" mode of proof —is often employed (even in Mathematics) for establishing what we maintain: that is, we prove the *falsity* of some Proposition (in other words, the *truth* of its *contradictory*) by showing that if assumed, as a Premise, along with another Premise known to be true, it leads to a Conclusion manifestly false. For though from a false assumption, either falsehood or truth may follow, from a true assumption, truth only can follow.

Let us now look to the case of a doubtful Premise. Suppose it admitted as *certain* that "a murderer deserves death," and as *probable* that "this man is a murderer," then, the Conclusion (that "he deserves death") is probable in exactly the same degree.

But though when one Premise is certain, and the other only probable, it is evident that the Conclusion will be exactly as probable as the *doubtful premise*, there is some liability to mistake, in cases where *each* Premise is merely probable. For though almost every one would perceive that in this case the probability of the Conclusion must be *less* than that of either Premise, the *precise degree* in which its probability is diminished, is not always so readily apprehended.

And yet this is a matter of exact and easy arithmetical calculation. I mean, that, *given* the probability of each Premise, we can readily calculate, and with perfect exactness, the probability of the Conclusion.

D

As for the probability of the Premises themselves that are put before us, that, of course, must depend on our knowledge of the *subject-matter* to which they relate. But supposing it agreed what the amount of probability is in each Premise, then we have only to state that probability in the form of a *fraction*, and to *multiply* the two fractions together, the product of which will give the degree of probability of the Conclusion.*

§ 4. Let the probability, for instance, of each Premise, be supposed the same; and let it in each, be $\frac{2}{3}$; [that is, let each Premise be supposed to have two to one in its favour; that is, to be twice as likely to be true as to be false;] then the probability of the Conclusion will be *two-thirds of two thirds;* that is, $\frac{4}{9}$;—rather less than one-half. For since twice two are four, and thrice three, nine, the fraction expressing the probability of the Conclusion will be four-ninths.

For example, suppose the Syllogism to be "A man who has the plague will die of it" (probably); "this man has the plague" (probably); therefore (probably) "he will die of it." We are—suppose—not certain of either Premise; though we think each to be probable: we have judged— suppose—that of 9 persons with the symptoms this man exhibits, two-thirds,—that is, six, have the plague: and again, that *two-thirds* of those who have the plague—that is, *four out of six*—die of it: then, of 9 persons who have these symptoms, 4 may be expected to die of the plague.

Again "Every X is Y ($\frac{3}{4}$); Z is X ($\frac{2}{3}$); therefore Z is Y $_{YZ}^{6}=\frac{1}{2}$); let the fractions written after each Premise express the degree of its probability: and the result will be that which is given as the probability of the Conclusion.

For instance, "A Planet without any atmosphere is uninhabited: the moon is a planet without any atmosphere; therefore the moon is uninhabited:" supposing these Propositions to be those represented in the former example (of X, Y, and Z) then the probability that "the moon is

---

* Those who are at all familiar with Arithmetic will hardly need to be reminded that,—since a *fraction* is *less* than a unit,—what is called (not strictly, but figuratively) *multiplying* anything by a fraction, means taking it *less than once;* so that for instance, $\frac{1}{2} \times \frac{2}{3}$ that is, a half multiplied (as is called) by two-thirds, means, two-thirds of a half; *i. e.* or $\frac{1}{3}$.

uninhabited," will be two-thirds of three-fourths; or one-half, since $\frac{2}{3}$ multiplied by three-fourths gives $\frac{6}{12}=\frac{1}{2}$.*

In the example just given, you will observe, that the probability of each Premise has been supposed *more* than $\frac{1}{2}$; that is, each has been assumed to be *more likely* to be true than not; and yet there is, for one of these Conclusions, only an even chance; and for the other less. The supposed patient is supposed to be rather *less* likely to die of the plague than not.

And, of course, when there is a *long train* of reasoning, —the conclusion of each argument being made one of the Premises of a succeeding one,—then, if a number of merely-probable Premises are introduced, the degree of probability diminishes at each successive stage.

And hence it may happen, in the case of a very long train of reasoning, that there may be but a slight probability for the ultimate Conclusion, even though the Premises successively introduced should be, some of them, quite certain, and the rest more probable than not.

And hence, we often have to employ several distinct trains of argument, each tending separately to establish some degree of probability in the Conclusion.

§ 5. When you have two (or more) distinct arguments, each, separately, establishing as probable the same con·clusion, the mode of proceeding to compute the total probability, is the *reverse* of that mentioned just above. For, there—in the case of two probable premises,—we consider what is the probability of their being *both* true; which is requisite, in order that the conclusion may be established by them. But, in the case of a conclusion *twice* (or oftener)

---

* Some persons profess contempt for all such calculations, on the ground that we cannot be *quite sure* of the exact *degree* of probability of each Premise. And it is true, that we are, in most cases, exposed to this unavoidable course of uncertainty; but this is no reason why we should not endeavour to guard against an *additional* uncertainty, which *can* be avoided. It is some advantage to have no *more* doubt as to the degree of probability of the Conclusion, than we have in respect to the Premises.

And in fact there are offices, kept by persons whose buisness it is, in which calculations of this nature are made, in the purchase of *contingent-reversions,* depending, sometimes, on a great variety of risks which can only be conjecturally estimated; and in effecting Insurances, not only against ordinary risks (the calculations of which are to be drawn from statistical-tables), but also against every variety and degree o *extra*-ordinary risks; the *exact* amount of which no one can confidently pronounce upon. But the calculations are based on the best estimate that can be formed.

proved probable by separate arguments, if these distinct indications of truth do not *all* of them *fail*, the conclusion is established. You consider, therefore, what is the probability of *both* these indications of truth being *combined* in favour of any conclusion that is *not* true.

Hence the mode of computation is, to state (as a fraction) the chances *against* the conclusion as proved by *each* argument; and to multiply these fractions together, to ascertain the chances against the conclusion as resting on *both* the arguments combined; and this fraction being subtracted from unity, the remainder will be the probability *for* the conclusion.

For instance, let the probability of a conclusion as established by a certain argument, be $\frac{1}{3}$: (suppose that this man is the perpetrator of a certain murder, from stains of blood being found on his clothes:) and again of the same conclusion as established by another argument, $\frac{1}{2}$: (suppose from the testimony of some witness of somewhat doubtful character:) then, the chances *against* the conclusion in each case, respectively, will be $\frac{2}{3}$ and $\frac{1}{2}$; which, multiplied together, give $\frac{2}{6}$ or $\frac{1}{3}$ *against* the conclusion. The probability, therefore, *for* the conclusion as depending on these *two* arguments jointly (*i. e.* that he is guilty of the murder) will be $\frac{2}{3}$, or two to one.*

As for the degree of probability of each Premise, *that,* as we have said, must depend on the subject-matter before us; and it would be manifestly impossible to lay down any fixed rules for judging of this. But it would be absurd to complain of the want of rules for determining a point for which it is plain no precise rules can be given; or to disparage, for that reason, such rules as *can* be given for the determining of another point. Mathematical Science will enable us—*given*, one side of a triangle and the adjacent angles,—to ascertain the other sides; and this is acknowledged to be something worth learning, although mathematics will not enable us to answer the question which is sometimes proposed in jest, "How long is a rope?"

Men are often misled in practice by not attending to these circumstances, plain as they are, when pointed out.

---

* See Lesson XVII., § 10.

§ 6. It has been already explained that the Maxim [or Dictum] applicable to every Argument when stated in the clearest form, is, that whatever is predicated universally of any term may be predicated in like manner [affirmed or denied, as the case may be] of whatever is comprehended under that term; and that this, consequently, is the "*Universal principle* of Reasoning."

And you may observe, that this Dictum [or Maxim] may, in fact, be regarded as merely the *most general* statement of "*An Argument*,"—not this or that individual argument; but *any and every* "Argument abstractedly."

For instance, if you say "This man is contemptible because he is a liar," you evidently mean to be understood, "Every liar is contemptible; this man is a liar; therefore he is contemptible." Now, if you so far *generalise* this Syllogism, as to omit all consideration of the very terms actually occurring in it, *abstracting*, and attending solely to the *form* of expression, you will have "Every X is Y; Z is X; therefore Z is Y;" and then if you proceed to make a still further abstraction, saying—instead of "Every X"—"*any-term-distributed*" and instead of "Y" —"anything whatever affirmed of that term," and so on, you will have, in substance, the very "Dictum" we have been speaking of: which may be separated into three portions, corresponding to the three Propositions of a Syllogism; thus,—

1. Anything whatever (as "Y") affirmed of a *whole class* (as "X").

2. under which class something else (as "Z") is comprehended.

3. may be affirmed of that (namely "Z") which is so comprehended.

These three portions, into which the Dictum has been separated, evidently answer to the Major-premise, Minor-premise, and Conclusion, of the Syllogism given above. And it is plain, that the like explanation will apply (if "denied" were put for "affirmed") to a Syllogism with a *negative* conclusion. So that the "Dictum" is in fact, as we have said, merely the most abstract and general form of stating the *Act of Reasoning*, universally.

§ 7. Some persons have remarked of this "Dictum" (meaning it as a disparagement) that it is merely a somewhat circuitous *explanation of what is meant by a Class.* It is in truth, just such an explanation of this as is needful to the student, and which must be kept before his mind in reasoning. For you are to recollect that not only every class [the Sign of which is, a "Common-term,"] comprehends under it an indefinite number of individuals—and often of other Classes—differing in many respects from each other, but also most of those individuals and classes may be referred, each to an indefinite number of classes (as was formerly explained), according as we *choose to abstract* this point or that from each.

Now to *remind* one, on each occasion, that so and so is referable to such and such a Class, and that the Class which happens to be before us comprehends such and such things,—this is *precisely all that is ever accomplished by Reasoning.*

For you may plainly perceive, on looking at any of the examples above, that when you assert both the Premises taken in conjunction, you have, virtually, implied the Conclusion. Else, indeed, it would *not* be impossible (as it is), for any one to deny the Conclusion, who admits both Premises.

§ 8. Hence, some have considered it as a disparagement to a Syllogism (which they imagine to be *one kind* of Argument) that you can gain no *new truth* from it ; the Conclusions it establishes being, in fact, known already by every one who has admitted the Premises.

Since, however, a Syllogism is not a certain distinct kind of argument, but *any* argument whatever, stated in a regular form, the complaint, such as it is, lies against Reasoning altogether.

And it is undeniable, that no *new truth*,—in one sense of the word—(and that, perhaps, the strictest sense) can ever be established by *Reasoning alone;* which merely unfolds as it were, and developes, what was, in a manner, wrapped up and implied in our previous knowledge ; but which we are often as much unaware of, to all practical purposes, till brought before us, as if it had been wholly beyond our reach.

New Truths,—in the strictest sense of the word—that is, such as are not implied in anything that was in our minds before,—can be gained only by the use of our senses, or from the reports of credible narrators, &c.

An able man may, by patient Reasoning, attain any amount of mathematical truths; because these are all implied in the Definitions. But no degree of labour and ability would give him the knowledge, by *"Reasoning"* *alone,* of what has taken place in some foreign country; nor would enable him to know, if he had never seen or heard of the experiments, what would become of a spoonful of salt or a spoonful of chalk if put into water, or what would be the appearance of a ray of light when passed through a prism.

§ 9. These two modes of arriving at any truth are perceived by all men as distinct. And they are recognised in the expressions in common use. The one is usually called *"information;"* the other *"instruction."** We speak of trusting to the *information* (not the *instruction*) of our senses. Any one who brings *news* from any place, or who describes some experiments he has witnessed, or some spot he has visited, is said to afford us *information.*

A Mathematician again, a Grammarian—a Moralist— any one who enters into a useful discussion concerning human life,—any in short who satisfactorily *proves* anything to us by *reasoning,*—is said to afford us *instruction.*

And in conversing with any one who speaks judiciously, one sometimes says "Very true!" or "That is a very just remark: that never struck me before," &c. In these and such like expressions, we imply both that what he says is not *superfluous,* but valuable and important, and also that we are conscious of having ourselves possessed, in our own previous knowledge, the germ of what he has developed, and the means of ascertaining the truth of what he has said; so as to have a right to bear *our testimony to it.*

But when any one gives us *information* about a foreign Country, &c., though we may fully *believe* him, and be interested by what he tells us, we never think of saying "Very true!" or "You are quite right." We readily per-

---

* It is not meant that this is the *only* sense of these words.

ceive that in this case the knowledge imparted is new to
us in quite another sense; and is what no *reasoning* alone
could have imparted; being not *implied* in anything we
knew already.

These two modes of attaining what are, in different
senses, new truths (and which, of course, are often *mixed*
together,) may be illustrated by two different modes in
which a man may obtain an addition to his wealth. One
man, suppose, has property to a certain value, *bequeathed*
to him; another *discovers* on his estate a mine of equal
value. Each of these is enriched to the same degree.
But the former of them acquires what he had, before, *no
right* to; the latter merely comes to the knowledge and
use of that which was before, legally, his property;
though, till discovered, it brought him no advantage.

Any mode of attaining knowledge, distinct from *Reasoning*, is, of course, foreign from the present inquiry.

LESSON XII.

§ 1. The Dictum [or Maxim] above explained as the
Universal-principle of Reasoning, will apply to a Syllo-
gism in such a form as that of the examples given.
"Every (or No) X is Y*; Z (whether some Z or every
Z) is X; therefore—some, or every—Z is Y;" or "No Z
is Y;" or "Some Z is not Y;" as the case may be.

And in that form every valid argument may be exhibited.

But there are other Syllogisms in other forms, to which
the "Dictum" cannot be *immediately* applied (though
they may be reduced into the above form), and which yet
are real Syllogisms, inasmuch as their conclusiveness is
manifest from the *form* of expression, independently of
the meaning of the Terms.

For instance, "No Savages have the use of metals; the
ancient Germans had the use of metals; therefore they
were not savages," is a valid Syllogism, though the
Dictum cannot be applied to it as here stated. But it
may readily be reduced into the form to which the Dictum

does apply; by illatively converting the Major-premise, into "men who have the use of metals are not Savages."

But the argument as it originally stood was a regular Syllogism; and so are some others also in a different form; although the Dictum does not *immediately* apply to them.

Accordingly, certain rules [or "Canons"] have been framed which do apply directly to *all* categorical Syllogisms, whether they are or are not in that form to which the Dictum is immediately applicable.

1st Canon. Two terms which *agree* with one and the same third, may be pronounced to agree with each other: and—

2nd Canon. Two terms whereof one *agrees* and the other *disagrees* with one and the same third, may be pronounced to disagree with each other.

The technical sense of the words "agree" and "disagree" has been explained in a former Lesson.

The two terms which are each compared with the same third, are the Terms [or " Extremes"] of the Conclusion; viz.: the Major-term and Minor-term: and that third Term with which they are separately compared in the two Premises, is the Middle-term.

On the former of these two Canons rests the proof of affirmative-conclusions; on the latter, of negative.

§ 2. To take first a Syllogism in the form originally given: " Every X is Y; Z is X; therefore Z is Y;" or again, " No X is Y; Z is X; therefore Z is not Y;" in these examples, " Y" and " Z" are, in the two Premises respectively, compared with " X:" in the former example they are assumed to *"agree"* with it; and thence in the Conclusion, they are pronounced (according to the 1st Canon) to "agree" with each other; in the latter example, " Y" is assumed to *"disagree"* with "X," and " Z" to "agree" with it; whence in the Conclusion they are pronounced (according to the 2nd Canon) to "disagree" with each other.

Again, to take a Syllogism in the other form, such as that in this Lesson, "No Savages," &c., or, "No Y is X; Z is X; therefore Z is not Y;" you will perceive that the 2nd Canon will apply equally well to this as to the preceding example.

You will also find, on examination of the apparent-syllogisms [fallacies]—of which examples were given in former Lessons, and whose faultiness was there explained, —that they transgress against the above "Canons."

. Take for instance, "*Some* X is Y; Z is X; therefore Z is Y:"* and again "Every Y is X; Z is X; therefore Z is Y;" or "Every tree is a vegetable; grass is a vegetable; therefore grass is a tree;" in these (as was formerly explained) the Middle-term is *undistributed;* [taken particularly in both Premises;] the two "Extremes," therefore, [Terms of the Conclusion] have been compared eaĉh with *part* only of the Middle; and thence we cannot say that they have each been compared with *one and the same third;* so that we are not authorized to pronounce their agreement or disagreement with each other.

But remember, that it is sufficient if the Middle-term be distributed in *one* of the Premises; since if one of the "Extremes" (of the Conclusion) has been compared with *part* of the "Middle," and the other with the *whole* of it, they have both been compared with the same; since the whole must include every part. And accordingly, in the form originally given "Every X is Y: Z is X," &c., you may observe that the Middle-term is distributed in the Major-premise, and undistributed in the Minor.

§ 3. Again, take the example formerly given, of "illicit process;" [proceeding from a term undistributed in the Premise, to the same, distributed, in the Conclusion;] as, "Every X is Y; Z is not X; therefore Z is not Y:" or, "Every tree is a vegetable; grass is not a tree; therefore grass is not a vegetable;" here the "Extremes" which in the Conclusion are compared together, are not really what had been compared, each with the Middle. For in the Conclusion, it is the *whole* of the term "vegetable" that is compared with the term "grass;" (since negatives distribute the Predicate,) though it was only PART of that term had been, in the Premise, compared with "tree;" the Predicate of an "Affirmative" being undistributed.

In this instance, therefore, as in the former one, the

---

* See the example from Hume, respecting Testimony.

Canons had not been complied with; each of these apparent-syllogisms having in reality four terms.

You will observe also, that when the Middle-term is
ambiguous, there are, in sense *two* Middle-terms, though
you may have, apparently, a correct Syllogism: as *"Light*
is opposite to darkness; feathers are *light;* therefore
feathers are opposite to darkness." The word "Light"
is here used *equivocally.* (See the explanation in Lesson
VII. § 3 of "univocal" and "equivocal.")

So glaring an equivocation as this, could, of course, deceive no one, and could only be applied in jest.* But when
there is a very *small* difference between the two senses in
which a Middle-term is used in the two Premises, then,
though the reasoning is not the less destroyed, the equivocation is the more likely to escape notice. And men are
practically deceived in this manner, every day, both by
others and by themselves.

§ 4. For instance, there is an argument of Hume's (in
the work referred to in a former example, and which is
said to have been convincing to some persons) which may
be regularly stated, thus: " Nothing that is contrary to
experience can be established by testimony; every miracle
is contrary to experience; therefore no miracle can be
established by testimony." Now the middle-term, *"contrary* to experience," admits of being understood in either
of two senses: sometimes (and this is the strict and proper
sense) it means "what we know by our own experience
to be false;" as, for instance, if several witnesses should
despose to some act having been done at a certain time
and place by a person known to me and in whose company
I was at the time, and in a different place, I should
be enabled to contradict their testimony from my own
experience.

Sometimes again the expression is employed to denote
"something which we have *never experienced,* and have
not known to be experienced by others;" which would
be the case with the ascent of a Balloon, for instance, to
one who had never seen or heard of such a thing; or with

---

* Most jests, it is to be observed,—such as puns, conundrums, &c.—are
mock fallacies.

the freezing of water, to a king of Bantam, mentioned by Hume.

Now, if the Term "contrary to experience" be understood in this latter sense in *both* Premises, then the *Major*-premise of the Syllogism will be manifestly false; since it would imply that the king of Bantam, or any one living in a hot country, could have no sufficient reason for believing in the existence of ice. And if the term be understood (in *both* Premises) in the other sense, then the *Minor* will be false; since a man cannot say that he *knows by his own experience* (whatever he may *believe* or *judge*, and however rightly) the falsity of every individual narrative of every alleged miracle.

But if the term is in each Premise to be so understood as that *each* shall be true, then it is evident that it must be taken as *two* different terms (in sense though not in sound) no less than the term "light" in the former example.

§ 5. As for the truth or falsity of any Premise, or the sense in which any term is to be understood, in this or that Proposition, of course no fixed rules can be given; as this must evidently be determined in each case, by the subject-matter we are engaged on.

But though no rules can be given for *detecting* and *explaining* every fallacious ambiguity, it is useful to learn and to keep in mind *where to seek* for it; namely, to look to the *Middle*-Term (the argument having been first stated in a syllogistic form) and to observe whether *that* is employed precisely in the same sense in each Premise.

As for the Terms of the *Conclusion*, there is not much danger of error or fallacy from any possible ambiguity in one of these; since in whatever sense either of these is employed in the Premise, it will naturally be understood in the Conclusion, in that same sense; though in itself, it might admit of other meanings.

If, for instance, any one should conclude that the "*Plantain*" is "worth cultivation in places where it will flourish, because it produces a vast amount of human food," you would understand him to mean both in the Premise and the Conclusion, the fruit-bearing "Plantain" of the West-Indies, and not the herb that grows in our fields.

Sometimes, however, in a long train of Reasoning, a person may be led into error, by remembering merely that a certain proposition *has* been proved, while he forgets *in what sense* it was proved.

§ 6. There are six rules commonly laid down, as resulting from the two Canons above-mentioned; by which rules any apparent Syllogism is to be tested; since none can be objected to which does not violate any of these rules; and any apparent-syllogism which does violate any of them, is not, in reality, conformable to the above Canons.

i. A Syllogism must have three, and only three Terms.

ii. It must have three, and but three Propositions.

iii. The Middle-term must be *one* only [*i. e.* not *double*], and therefore must be *unequivocal*, and must be, (in one at least of the Premises,) *distributed*.

iv. No term is to be distributed in the Conclusion that was not distributed in the Premise: [or, there must be no "illicit-process."]

v. One at least of the Premises must be affirmative; since, if both were negative, the Middle-term would not have been pronounced either to agree with each of the "Extremes," or to agree with one and disagree with the other; but to *disagree* with *both;* whence nothing can be inferred : as, "No X is Y ; and Z is not X," evidently affords no ground for comparing Y and Z together.

And vi. If one premise be *negative*, the *Conclusion* must be negative: since—inasmuch as the other Premise must be affirmative—the middle will have been assumed to agree with one of the "Extremes," and to disagree with the other.

All these rules will have been sufficiently explained in what has already been said.

And from these you will perceive, that in every Syllogism one Premise at least must be universal; since if both were Particular, there would be either an undistributed Middle, or an Illicit-process.

For if each Premise were I (Particular-affirmative) there would be no distribution of any Term at all ; and if the Premises were I and O, there would be but one Term,— the Predicate of O [the Particular-negative]—distributed ; and supposing that one to be the Middle, then the Conclusion (being of course *negative*, by rule vi.) would have its Predicate—the Major-term—distributed, which had not been distributed in the Premise. Thus, "Some X is Y; some Z is not X," or again "some X is not Y; some Z is X," would prove nothing.

And for the like reasons, if one of the Premises be Particular, you can only infer a Particular Conclusion: as "every X is Y; some Z is X," will only authorize you to conclude, "Some Z is Y," since to infer a Universal would be an *"illicit-process of the Minor Term."*

§ 7. What is called the *"Mood"* [or "Mode"] of a Syllogism, is the designation of the three Propositions it contains (in the order in which they stand) according to their respective Quantity and Quality; that is, according as each Proposition is A, E, I, or O.

Looking merely to the arithmetical calculation of *permutations* (as it is called), all the possible combinations of the four Symbols, by threes, would amount to 64. For each of the 4 admits of being combined, in *pairs*, with each of the 4: [as A with A, with E, with I, and with O; &c.] which gives 16 pairs; and each of these 16 pairs admits of being combined with each of the 4 as a third; which gives $16 \times 4 = 64$.

But it is plain that several of these combinations are such as could not take place in a Syllogism. For instance, E, O, O, could not be a Mood of any Syllogism, since it would have *negative-premises* (see rule v.), nor I, O, O, which would have both premises *particular*, nor I, E, O, which would have an illicit process of the Major-term; since the Conclusion being negative would have the Major-term distributed, while the Major-premise, being I, would have no term distributed, and so with many others.

There will be found, on examination, to be in all only eleven Moods, in which any Syllogism can be expressed: and these are, A, A, A,—E, A, E,—A, I, I,—E, I, O,— A, E, E,—A, O, O,—A, A, I,—I, A, I—E, A, O,—O, A, O,—A, E, O.

§ 8. What is called the *"Figure"* of a Syllogism, is the *situation of the Middle-term*, in the two Premises respectively, with relation to the two "Extremes" [or Terms] of the Conclusion,—the Major and Minor Terms.

It is evident that all the possible collocations of the Middle must be four; since it must be either the Subject of the Major-premise and the predicate of the Minor; or the Predicate of each; or the Subject of each; or the Predicate of the Major and Subject of the Minor.

On looking to the examples originally given, you will see that a Syllogism in that form ["Every X is Y; Z is X; therefore Z is Y"] has the *Middle-term made the Subject of the Major-premise*, and the *Predicate of the Minor*.

This is called the *First Figure*; and it is to Syllogisms in this figure alone that the "*Dictum*" above-mentioned will *at once* apply.

§ 9. If you look to the form afterwards exemplified: (§ 1 of this Lesson) as "No savages, &c." or "No Y is X; Z is X; therefore Z is not Y," you will see that the Middle is the *Predicate of each* Premise. This is called the *Second Figure*. And in this, evidently none but *negative* Conclusions can be proved; since one of the Premises must be *negative*, in order that the Middle-term may be (by being the *Predicate* of a *Negative*) distributed.

Again, the Middle-term may be the *Subject of each* Premise. And this is called the *Third Figure*. Thus "Some X is Y; every X is Z; therefore some Z is Y;" is a correct Syllogism in the Third Figure, being conformable to the first *Canon*.

And the Syllogism here given as an example may be easily reduced to the First Figure, by simply converting the Major-premise, and taking it for the *Minor*; [*transposing* the Premises;] which will enable you to infer the simple-converse of the Conclusion: as "Every X is Z; some Y is X; therefore some Y is Z:" and this implies that "some Z is Y;" since (as was explained formerly) the simple conversion of I is *illative*.

For instance, "some painful things are salutary; every thing painful is an object of dread: therefore some things which are objects of dread are salutary;" this, though a valid Syllogism as it stands, may be reduced, in the manner above stated, to the First Figure.

In this, or in other ways, any Syllogism in the Third Figure may be easily "*reduced*" (as the technical phrase is) to the First Figure.

In this Third Figure you will find that none but *Particular* Conclusions can be drawn. To infer a Universal would always, you will find, involve an "*illicit process* of the Minor-term." For if the Premises are both Universal, (which as we have already seen (§ 6) they must always be, to warrant a Universal Conclusion,) then, supposing them to be A, A, there will have been,—in this Third Figure—no term distributed except the Middle; (affirmatives not distributing the Predicate;) and consequently no term can be distributed in the Conclusion; which must therefore be I.

And if the Premises be E and A, there will have been (besides the middle) only one term,—the Predicate of E, distributed; and consequently only one term can be distributed in the Conclusion; and that one must be the Predicate of O; since the Universal [E] would have *both* terms distributed.

§ 10. The Third Figure might be called the "*exceptive*" or the "*refutatory*" Figure; (or, agreeably to the expression of the Greek writers, the "*enstatic*;") as being a very natural form of expressing arguments which go to establish the *contradictory of some Universal* Proposition that any one may have maintained, or that may be generally believed.

For instance, if any one were speaking of "metals" as being, *universally*, "conductors of heat," you might *adduce* "Platina" as an *exception*. Or should any one contend that "no agent incapable of distinguishing moral good and evil (as for instance a madman) can be deterred from any act by apprehension of punishment," you might refute this, by adducing the case of a brute,—for instance, a dog—deterred from sheep-biting by fear of punishment. And such arguments would fall very naturally into the Third Figure.

It is, especially, the most natural form in which to express an argument—such as we often employ for the above purpose—in which the Middle-term is a *Singular*-term; as when, for instance, you prove, by the example of a certain individual,[*] the contradictory of a proposition (which would seem to most persons a very probable conjecture)

---

[*] See the Note on a former Lesson, on the case of Laura Bridgeman.

that a deaf and dumb person, born blind, cannot be taught *language*.

The Second Figure may be called the *"exclusive"* Figure; being a very natural form for arguments used in any inquiry in which we go on *excluding*, one by one, certain suppositions, or certain classes of things, from that whose description we are seeking to ascertain.

Thus, certain symptoms, suppose, exclude, *"Small Pox;"* that is, prove this *not* to be the patient's disorder; other symptoms, suppose, exclude *"Scarlatina,"* &c., and so one may proceed, by gradually narrowing the range of possible suppositions.

These three Figures are the only ones in which any argument would, designedly, be stated. For, as to *what* is called the Fourth Figure (in which the Middle-term is made the Predicate of the Major-premise and the Subject of the Minor) though a Syllogism so stated would be undeniably valid if conformable to the rules (as "every Y is X; no X is Z; therefore no Z is Y"), this form is only a clumsy and *inverted* way of stating what would naturally be expressed in the First Figure; as, in this example, might be done by transposing the Premises, and simply converting the Conclusion.

LESSON XIII.

§ 1. Besides *Categorical*-arguments, which we have been treating of, Reasoning is often expressed in a *Hypothetical* form. And though such arguments may be reduced into categorical form, this is not necessary, except for the purpose of pointing out the *sameness* in all cases of the Reasoning-process. For you may exhibit in a hypothetical form a perfect *"Syllogism"* as above defined.

A Hypothetical (or as some writers call it, a "compound") Proposition, consists of "two or more Categorical propositions, united by a Conjunction, in such a manner as to make them *one* proposition." And the different kinds of hypothetical-proposition are named after their respective Conjunctions; namely, "Conditional" and

"Disjunctive."* For instance, "if A is B, then X is Y," is a Conditional-Proposition;† "either A is B, or X is Y" is Disjunctive.

And each of these is a real *Proposition*, *i.e. asserts* something; and consequently is either *true* or *false;* which (as was formerly explained) is peculiar to *Propositions;* and each is also *one* Proposition, though consisting of several parts [or "members"] each of which if taken separately would be itself a proposition; but the Conjunction (which is called the Copula) makes the whole *one* Proposition.

§ 2. For instance, "the world is eternal," is a proposition; "records earlier than the Mosaic exist," is another proposition; and "*if* the world be eternal, records earlier than the Mosaic must exist," is a third proposition distinct from each of the others, and which may be true, though they be both false; since it does not assert the *truth* of either of them, but only the *connexion* between them. Again, should any one say "if the Northern-lights be shining, some great revolution of an empire is going on," this would be, properly speaking, a false Proposition, even should it turn out that each of the "members" stated as a categorical proposition is true; supposing it admitted that they have no *connexion* with each other.

Observe, however, that no *false conclusion* can be deduced from a false Conditional-proposition, when it so happens that both its "members" (stated as categorical-propositions) are true.

In the case of a Disjunctive-proposition, on the other hand, it is implied, that one at least of *its* "members" (stated as a categorical-proposition) must be true, and that if not, the whole proposition must be false. As, "this man was either at Oxford or at Cambridge" would not be true, if he were *not* at Oxford, *and not* at Cambridge.

And it is usually meant to be understood that *only* one of the members can be true; for if this were not the meaning in such an example as the foregoing, it would have been more correct to say "this man was either at Oxford, or Cambridge, or *both.*"

---

† Those writers who use the word *compound*-proposition instead of *hypothetical*, employ "hypothetical" to signify "conditional."

§ 3. A Hypothetical-*syllogism*, is one in which the *reasoning itself turns on the Hypothesis;* not, every syllogism that *has in it* a hypothetical premise; for the "hypothesis" may be a portion of one of the Terms, and the syllogism may be merely categorical.

For instance, "Real miracles are evidence of a divine commission ; if the works of Jesus were acknowledged miraculous by the unbelieving Jews, they must have been real miracles ; therefore the works of Jesus (if they were acknowledged, &c.,) are evidence of a divine commission;" is a categorical syllogism; the hypothesis being merely a portion of the Minor-term.

And so also with such an example as " Every X is either Y or W ; Z is X ; therefore Z is either Y or W."

In a hypothetical-syllogism, properly so called,—that is, in which the reasoning is based on a hypothetical premise, that premise is called the *Major*, and the other— which is categorical—is called the Minor-premise.

We will first speak of *Conditional*-syllogisms.

There are, in a Conditional-proposition, *two* members [categorical propositions] whereof one is asserted to *depend* on the other. That on which the other depends is called the " *Antecedent ;*" that which depends on it, the "*Consequent;*" and the *connexion* between the two, (expressed by "if" or "supposing,") is called the " *consequence.*"

(Consequence)   (Antecedent)

For instance " If————this man is a murderer———

(Consequent)   (Consequent)

he deserves death." " The English are well off———

(Consequence)   (Antecedent)

———if——they know their own advantages."

The natural order is to place the " Antecedent" *first ;* but this (as you will see from the example above) is not essential.

§ 4. The meaning, then, of a Conditional proposition, is, that "the *Antecedent* being assumed to be *true*, the *Consequent* is to be granted as true also." And this may be considered in two points of view : 1st, allowing that the Antecedent *is* true, the Consequent *must* be true ; 2ndly, supposing the Antecedent *were* true, the Consequent *would* be true.

Hence, there are two kinds of Conditional-syllogism ; 1st, if the Antecedent be (in the minor-premise) granted to be true, the Consequent may (in the Conclusion) be inferred : 2ndly, if the Consequent be *not* true—that is, if its *Contradictory* be assumed in the minor-premise—the Antecedent cannot be true ; that is, its Contradictory may, in the Conclusion, be inferred : since if the Antecedent *had been* true, the Consequent (which we have assumed to be false) *would have been* true also.

A Syllogism of the former kind, is called *"Constructive,"* of the latter kind *"Destructive."*

For instance, if "A is B, X is Y:" let this be the major-premise; then, if you add, "but A is B ; therefore X is Y," this forms a Constructive-syllogism ; if you say "X is not Y ; therefore A is not B;" this is a Destructive-syllogism. Thus "if this river has tides, the sea into which it flows must have tides;" then if I add "this river has tides," it follows in Conclusion, that "the sea into which it flows has tides ;" which is a Constructive-syllogism. If I add "the sea into which it flows has no tides," it follows that "this river has no tides."

§ 5. And here observe, by the way, that in hypothetical-arguments we are not concerned with the distinction between *affirmative and negative Conclusions.* For, of the two members of a Conditional-Proposition, either, or both, may be affirmative, or may be negative ; so that we may establish the truth "constructively" of either an affirmative or a negative Consequent ; or may ("destructively") establish the falsity—that is, infer the Contradictory—of either an affirmative or negative Antecedent.

For instance, "if no miracles had been displayed by the first preachers of the Gospel, they could not have obtained a hearing; but they did obtain a hearing ; therefore some miracles must have been displayed by them ;" is a Destructive-conditional-Syllogism.

The Consequent, as has been said, depends on the Antecedent ; so that, if the Antecedent be true, the Consequent will be true also ; but as the Antecedent does not depend on the Consequent, nothing is proved by *denying* the Antecedent, or again, by *assuming* the *truth* of the Consequent. Suppose it granted, that "if A is B, X is Y," though it may indeed so happen that X is Y, *only* on *that* condition,—that is, that if X is Y, A is B,—this is not implied by the original assertion; so that (merely assuming that original assertion), to add that "A is not B," or again, to say " X is Y," proves nothing.

For instance, "if this man has committed theft, he deserves punishment," does not authorize me to proceed either to say "he has not committed theft; therefore he does not deserve punishment;" or again, "he deserves punishment; therefore he has committed theft." For it is (in this case) evident that a man may deserve punishment·for some other offence.

§ 6. And you may observe, that the fallacy of *affirming the Consequent* and thence inferring the truth of the Antecedent, answers to the fallacy (in Categoricals) of *undistributed-middle* or to that of *negative-premises;* as may be seen from the above example. For to say, "every one who has committed theft deserves punishment; and this man deserves punishment," would evidently be a case of undistributed Middle. And again, if instead of saying "if this man has a fever he is not fit to travel; and he is not fit to travel ; therefore he has a fever," you say "no one who has a fever is fit to travel," &c., there will be the fallacy of two negative-premises.

The fallacy again of denying the Antecedent, and thence inferring the denial of the Consequent, would correspond (in Categoricals) either to an "illicit-process of the Major-term," or to the Fallacy of "two negative-premises," or that of introducing palpably "more than three terms." For instance, suppose instead of saying " If this man has committed theft," &c. you say, " Every one who has committed theft deserves punishment; this man has not committed theft," &c. this would be an illicit-process of the Major. Or again, suppose, instead of saying, "If this man has a fever, he is not fit to travel; but he has not a fever ; therefore he is fit to travel," you say, "No one who has a fever is fit to travel ; this man has not a fever," &c., this would be to employ "two negative-premises." Again, "If this army is not brave it will not be victorous; it is brave; therefore it will be victorious;" would, if expressed categorically, have palpably more than three terms.

§ 7. It is plain, from what has been above said, that a Conditional-proposition may be illatively *converted*, by taking the *Contradictory of the Consequent for an Antecedent* and (of course) the Contradictory of the Antecedent for a Consequent. "If A is B, X is Y," implies that "if X is not Y, A is not B." "If all wages be regulated by the price of food, an English labourer will have higher wages than an American;" this manifestly implies, that, "if an English labourer has not higher wages than an American, all wages are not regulated by the price of food.

This corresponds to the conversion of the categorical-proposition A, "by negation;" ["contraposition;"] every Conditional-proposition corresponding in fact to a Universal-affirmative-Categorical; the *Antecedent* answering to the *Subject;* and the *Consequent*, to the *Predicate*.

It is evident, that if you thus convert the Major-premise [the hypothetical-premise] of any Conditional-syllogism, you change the Syllogism from "*Constructive*" to "*Destructive*," or vice versâ from Destructive to Constructive.

The Proposition "if A is B, X is Y" may be considered as amounting to this; "The case [or supposition] of A being B, is a case of X being Y." And then to say (as in the Minor-premise and the Conclusion, of a constructive-conditional syllogism) "A is B; and therefore X is Y;" is equivalent to saying "the present [or the existing] case is a case of A being B; therefore this is a case of X being Y."

Or again, "if the Stoics are right, pain is no evil; but pain is an evil; therefore the Stoics are not right," (which is a destructive-conditional syllogism,) may be reduced to a Categorical, thus: "To say that pain is no evil——is not——true; to say that the Stoics are right——is ————to say that pain is no evil; therefore to say that the Stoics are right——is not——true."

This Syllogism is in the First Figure. The argument might be exhibited in the Third Figure, thus: "that pain is no evil is not true; but that is maintained by the Stoics; therefore something maintained by the Stoics is not true."

In some such way (taking care always to preserve the *same sense*) any argument may be exhibited in various different *forms* of expression, (the choice of which is merely a matter of convenience,) so as to point out and impress on

the mind that the reasoning-process itself is always essen-
tially one and the same, and may ultimately be referred
to the "Dictum" formerly mentioned.

§ 8. In a disjunctive proposition, as has been already
observed, it is implied, *that at least some one of the "members" must be true.* If therefore *all except one* be (in the
Minor-premise) denied, the truth of the remaining one
may be inferred.

For instance, "either the Gospel was an invention of
impostors, or it was a dream of fanatics, or a real revelation; it was neither of the two former; therefore it
was a real revelation."

But if there be more than two members, and you deny
(in the Minor-premise) one or more of them, but not *all
except one*, then you can only draw a *disjunctive* Conclusion:
as, " this event occurred either in Spring, Summer, Autumn,
or Winter ; it did not occur in Summer or in Winter ;
therefore it occurred either in Spring or in Autumn."

In a disjunctive-proposition it is (as has been said above)
usually understood that the members are *exclusive; i. e.*
that *only one* of them can be true ; and you may, on that
supposition, infer from the *truth* of one of them (assumed
in the Minor) the Contradictory of the other, or others.
As "either A is B, or C is D, or X is Y: but A is B ;
therefore C is not D, nor is X Y."

§ 9. A Disjunctive-syllogism may readily be reduced to
a *Conditional*, by merely altering the form of the Major
premise; namely, by taking as an *Antecedent* the Contradictory of one or more of the members; everything else
remaining as before. Thus, in the example lately given,
you might say "*If* this did not occur in Summer, nor
in Winter, it must have occurred either in Spring or in
Autumn;" &c.

A Disjunctive-proposition, you are to observe, is, (as
well as a Conditional,) always *affirmative*. For, either kind
of Hypothetical proposition always *affirms* the *connexion*
of the members of it, [categorical-propositions contained in
it,] whether these be affirmative or negative propositions.

And the *contradiction* of a Hypothetical-proposition must
therefore consist in *denying* this *connexion;* which is done,
not in a Hypothetical, but in a Categorical proposition.

When it is asserted, that "if A is B, X is Y" you would contradict this by saying " it does not *follow that* if A is B, X must be Y ;" or by some such expression.   Or when it is asserted that " either A is B, or X is Y," you might contradict this, by saying "*it is possible that* neither A is B, nor X Y ;" or you might contradict a Disjunctive-proposition by two or more Categorical propositions ; namely, by asserting separately the Contradictory of each member; as " either some Z is Y, or else some W is not X," might be contradicted by " no Z is Y, and every W is X."

LESSON XIV.

§ 1. It will often happen, that you will have occasion to employ that complex kind of Conditional-syllogism (consisting of two or more such syllogisms *combined*) which is commonly called a " *Dilemma.*"

When you have before you as admitted truths two (or more) Conditional-propositions, with different Antecedents, but each with the same Consequent, and these Antecedents are such that you cannot be sure of the truth of any *one* of them separately, but are sure that *one* or *other* must be true, you will then naturally be led to state *both* of the Conditional-propositions first ; and next, to assert *disjunctively* the Antecedents ; and thus to infer the common Consequent.   As " if every A is B, X is Y; and if some A is not B, X is Y; but either every A is B, or some A is not B ; therefore X is Y."

This kind of argument was urged by the opponents of Don Carlos, the pretender to the Spanish Throne ; which he claimed as heir-male, against his niece the queen, by virtue of the Salic law excluding females ; which was established (contrary to the ancient Spanish usage) by a former king of Spain, and was repealed by King Ferdinand.   They say, " if a king of Spain has a right to alter the law of succession Carlos has no claim ; and if no king of Spain has that right, Carlos has no claim ; but a king of Spain either has or has not, such right; therefore (on either supposition) Carlos has no claim."

§ 2. When several Conditional-propositions have different Consequents as well as different Antecedents, then we can only *disjunctively* infer those Consequents: that is, we can only infer that (supposing some one or other of the Antecedents true) *one* or *other* of the Consequents must be true. As "if A is B, X is Y; and if C is D, P is Q; but either A is B, or C is D; therefore either X is Y, or P is Q." Thus "if the obedience due from Subjects to Rulers extends to religious worship, the ancient Christians are to be censured for refusing to worship the heathen idols; if the obedience, &c., does not so extend, no man ought to suffer civil penalties on account of his religion; but the obedience, &c., either does so extend, or it does not; therefore either the ancient Christians are to be censured, &c., or else no man ought to suffer civil penalties on account of his religion."

So also, "if a man is capable of rising, unassisted, from a savage to a civilized state, some instances may be produced of a race of savages having thus civilized themselves; and if Man is not capable of this, then, the first rudiments of civilization must have originally come from a superhuman instructor; but either Man is thus capable, or not; therefore either some such instance can be produced, or the first rudiments," &c.

§ 3. And when there are several Antecedents each with a different Consequent, then, we may have a Destructive-dilemma: that is, we may, in the Minor-premise *disjunctively deny* the Consequents, and in the Conclusion disjunctively deny the Antecedents. Or again, you may have a Dilemma partly Constructive and partly Destructive; that is, in the Minor-premise (which in a Dilemma is always a disjunctive-proposition) the members—suppose for instance there are two,—may be, one of them, the assertion of the Antecedent of one of the Conditional-propositions, and the other, the contradictory of the Consequent of the other Conditional.

Suppose we say, "if X is not Y, A is not B; and if P is not Q, C is not D; but either A is B, or C is D; therefore either X is Y, or P is Q;" this would be a Destructive-Dilemma; and you may see that it corresponds exactly with the example given a little above, only that we

E

have, here, *converted* both of the Conditional-propositions.
(See § 7 of the preceding Lesson).   If we had converted
one only, and not the other, of the Conditionals (as "if A
is B, X is Y; and if P is not Q, C is not D ;" &c.), then
the Dilemma would have been *partly* Constructive, and
partly *Destructive*.   For, as has been formerly explained,
the Difference between a Constructive and Destructive
Syllogism consists merely in the form of expression, and
it is very easy to reduce either form into the other.

It may be worth while to observe, that it is very common to state the *Minor*-premise of a Dilemma first ; in
order to show the more clearly that the several Categorical
propositions which are, each, doubtful, when taken separately, may be combined into a Disjunctive-proposition
that admits of no doubt.   And this Minor-premise being
disjunctive, some have hence been led to suppose that a
Dilemma is a kind of *disjunctive* argument ; though it is
really, as we have shown, a *Conditional*.

The name of "*D*ilemma," again, has led some to suppose that it must consist of *two* members only; though it
is evident that there may be any number.

§ 4.   When there is a long Series of arguments, the
Conclusion of each being made one of the Premises of the
next, till you arrive at your ultimate Conclusion, it is of
course a tedious process to exhibit the whole in the form
of a series of Syllogisms. This process may, in many cases,
be considerably abridged, without departing from the
strict syllogistic form : [that is, such a form as shows the
conclusiveness of the reasoning, from the *expression
alone*, independently of the meaning of the Terms, and
equally well when arbitrary Symbols are used to stand
for the Terms].

What is called a "Sorites" (from a Greek word signifying a *heap*, or *pile*) is such an abridged form of stating a
train of arguments.   When you state a series of propositions in which the Predicate of the first is made the Subject (distributed) of the next, and the Predicate of that,
again, in like manner, the Subject of the next, and so on,
to any length, you may then predicate in the Conclusion,
the *Predicate*) of the *last* Premise of the Subject of the
first.

Thus "A (either "some" or "every") is B; every B is C; every C is D ; every D is E; &c., therefore A is E ;" or " no D is E ; therefore A is not E." Thus also, " this man is selfish ; whoever is selfish is neglectful of the good of others ; whoever is neglectful of the good of others is destitute of friends ; and whoever is destitute of friends is wretched ; therefore this man is wretched."

§ 5. To such a form of argumentation the " Dictum" formerly treated of, may be applied, with one small addition, which is self-evident. Whatever is affirmed or denied of a whole Class, may be affirmed or denied of whatever is comprehended in [*any class that is wholly comprehended in*] that Class." This sentence, omitting the portion enclosed in brackets, you will recognise as the "Dictum" originally laid down: and the words in brackets supply that extension of it which makes it applicable to a " Sorites," of whatever length; since it is manifest that that clause might be enlarged, as far as you will, into "a Class that is wholly comprehended in a class, which again is wholly comprehended in another Class," &c.

You will perceive, on looking at the above examples, that, though the first of the propositions of a Sorites may be either Universal or Particular, all the succeeding Premises must be *Universal ;* since, else, the " Dictum," as stated just above, would not apply.

You will perceive also that though the last of the Premises may be either Negative or Affirmative, all the preceding ones must be *Affirmative,* in order that the Dictum may be applicable. Thus, in the example first given, it is allowable to say " no D is E : therefore A is not E ;" but then it is necessary that "C" should be *comprehended* in "D" (not *excluded* from it) and "B" likewise in "C" and "A" in "B," since otherwise the " Dictum " would not be applicable.

§ 6. It will be seen, on examining the examples, that there are in a Sorites as many Middle-terms as there are *intermediate* propositions between the first and the last ; and that it may be stated in just so many separate syllogisms in the First Figure ; which is the simplest and most common form of a Syllogism.

The first of these Syllogisms will have for its *Major*-premise the *second* of the propositions in the series, and for its *Minor*-premise, the first of them ; and the Conclusion of this first syllogism will be a proposition which is (in the Sorites) not expressed but understood ; and which will be the Minor-premise of the next Syllogism. And of this next syllogism the Major-premise will be the *third* that is expressed in the Sorites ; and so on.

For instance (1st), "every B is C ; A is B ;" ["therefore A is C"] ; (2ndly), "every C is D ;" ["A is C ; therefore A is D"], &c.   .

The portions enclosed in brackets are those which in the Sorites are *understood*.

The *only Minor*-premise expressed in the Sorites is the first proposition of the Series; all the succeeding Minor-premises being understood.

And hence it is that (as has been above said) this first is the only one of all the Premises that may allowably be a *Particular :* because, in the first Figure, though the Minor may be either Universal or Particular, the *Major* (as you see from what was formerly said of the "Dictum"), must always be *Universal ;* and *all* the premises in the Sorites, except the first, are *Major*-premises.

In this way may also be explained what was above said, that the *last* of the premises of a Sorites is the only one that can allowably be a *Negative ;* since if any of the others were negative, the result would be that one of the Syllogisms of the Series would have a negative Minor-premise; which in the first Figure (as you will see by again referring to the " Dictum") is inadmissible.

§ 7. A Series of *Conditional*-syllogisms (which correspond, as has been shown, to Categorical-syllogisms in the first Figure) may in like manner be abridged into a Sorites; by making the Consequent of the first proposition the Antecedent of the next; and so on: and then drawing the Conclusion by either asserting the *first* Antecedent, and thence (constructively), inferring the last Consequent, or else, denying the *last* of the Consequents, and (destructively) inferring the Contradictory of the first Antecedent. As "if A is B, C is D; and if C is D, E is F; and if E is F, G is H," &c.: and then if the Sorites be "Constructive," you add "but A is B, therefore G is H ;" or, if "destructive," but " G is not H ; therefore A is not B."

The foregoing are all the forms in which Reasoning can be exhibited *Syllogistically; i. e.* so that its validity shall be manifest from the *mere form of expression.*

For, an *Enthymeme* (see Lesson II. § 3) is manifestly not syllogistic; since it is possible to admit the truth of the one premise that is expressed, and yet to deny the Conclusion.

An Enthymeme may indeed be such (since it contains all the three Terms requisite for a Syllogism,) that we can readily perceive what the premise is that *ought* to be understood, and which, *if* supplied, would make the Syllogism complete: as " Z is X ; therefore Z is Y ;" [or " the Elk has horns on the head ; therefore it is a ruminant :"] this *would* be syllogistic, *if* you were to prefix " Every X is Y ;" but whether this be the Premise *actually meant* to be understood, we can only judge from the sense of the words that are expressed, and from what we believe respecting the subject-matter in hand, and the design of the speaker.

In a Syllogistic form, on the other hand—whether Categorical or Hypothetical, and whether at full length, or abridged into a Sorites—that which is *actually expressed* in the Premises is such that no one *can possibly suppose these true* (whatever be the *meaning of the Terms* or whether we *understand* them or not) *without admitting the truth of the Conclusion* thence drawn.

§ 8. As for any arguments that are *not* expressed in a regular form, of course no precise rules can be laid down for reducing them into such a form; since any arguments to which such rules do apply must evidently be, on that very ground, pronounced to be *already* syllogistic. Some general remarks, however, (drawn chiefly from what has been taught in the foregoing Lessons,) may be practically serviceable in the operation of reducing arguments into regular form.

i. It has been remarked (in Lesson III. § 7), that men are very impatient of tedious prolixity in Reasoning; and that the utmost *brevity,*—the most *compressed* statement of argumentation,—that is compatible with clearness,—is always aimed at, and is indeed *conducive* to clearness. And hence (as was pointed out), a single sentence,—or even a word—will often be a sufficient *hint* of an entire syllogism.

And it may be added, that such a sentence will sometimes be in the form, not of a *Proposition*, but of an *Exclamation*,—a *Question*,—or a *Command ;* and yet will be such as readily to suggest to the mind a Proposition.

For instance, in some of the examples lately given, one might say (in the place of one of the Propositions) "Choose which you will of these two suppositions ;" or "who can doubt that so and so follows?"

The message to Pilate from his wife* furnishes an instance of a single word *("just")* suggesting a Major-premise, while the Conclusion is stated in the form of an *exhortation:* "Have thou nothing to do with that *just* man." And the succeeding sentence must have been designed to convey a hint of Arguments for the proof of each of the Premises on which that Conclusion rested.

§ 9. ii. Remember that (as was formerly shown) we may change any proposition from Affirmative to Negative, or vice versâ, without altering the sense: it being the same thing, for instance, to *affirm* of any one the term "not happy," or to deny "happy." So that an argument may be valid which might appear at the first glance to have "negative-premises."

But if the above experiment be tried in an argument that is *really* faulty on that ground, the only effect will be, to change one fallacy into another: as "A covetous man is not happy; this man is not covetous; therefore he is happy;" here, if you take "happy" as the predicate of the Major, you have negative-premises: if you take "not happy" [or "unhappy"] as the term, you will have *four terms.*

On the other hand, "no one is happy who is not content; no covetous man is content; therefore no covetous man is happy," is a valid syllogism.

That the Conversion-by-negation [contra-position] of a Universal-affirmative is *illative,* has been formerly explained. And it is very common, and often conducive to clearness, to state such a proposition (Λ) in the form of this its converse (E); as, for instance, instead of "every motive that could have induced this man to act so and so, must have been purely benevolent," to say, "no motive but pure benevolence could have induced him to act so."

iii. Remember that one single sentence (as was formerly explained, Lesson IX. § 7) may imply several distinct propositions, according to the portions of it which you understand as the Subject, and as the Predicate. For instance, " It is the duty of the Judge to decide for him who is in the right; this plaintiff is in the right; therefore it is the Judge's duty to decide for him," might be understood as having *five terms:* but according to the *drift* of the first premise (considered as a part of this argument) what you are speaking of is, not " the duty of the Judge," but " the person who is in the right;" of whom you assert that "he is fairly entitled to the Judge's decision on his side."   And if thus stated, the argument will be seen to be valid.

And here it may be remarked, that to state distinctly as Subject and Predicate, that which is *really spoken of,* and that which *is said of* it, will be often the best and most effectual exposure of a Fallacy; which will always be the more likely to escape detection, the more *oblique* and *involved* is the expression.

PART III.

SUPPLEMENT.

LESSON XV.

---

§ 1. There are some other technical terms, which it is useful to be familiar with, and which we will therefore now proceed to treat of in a supplementary Lesson. They are such as are usually introduced in an earlier place, previously to the matter of the last five Lessons. But it has been thought better to postpone everything that was not indispensable for the right understanding of what has been said concerning the several forms of Syllogism.

A "Common-term," we have seen, is so called from its expressing what is *common* to several things: and is thence called also a "Predicable," inasmuch as it can be affirmatively-*predicated*, in the same sense ["univocally"] of certain other terms. It is evident, that the word "Predicable" is *relative*, i. e. denotes the *relation* in which some Term stands to some other, *of* which it can be predicated. And this relation is of different kinds; in other words there are several *Classes* [or Heads] of Predicables.

When you are asked concerning any individual thing, "*What* is it?" the answer you will give, if strictly correct, would be what is technically called its "Species;" as, "this is a *pen*;" "that is a *man*;" "this is a *circle*;" "that is a *magnet*," &c.

And the "Species" of anything is usually described in technical language as expressing its "whole essence;" meaning the whole of what *can* be expressed by a *Common*-term: for it is plain that (as was formerly shown) it is only by taking an *inadequate* view of an "Individual," so as to *abstract* from it what is common to it with certain other individuals, disregarding all that distinguishes it from them (including its *actual existence* as a single object)—it is only then, I say, that we can obtain any Common-term.

§ 2. When the same question "What is this?" is asked respecting a *Species*, the term by which you answer, is, that Predicable which is technically called the "*Genus*" of that

Species.   As, "What is a *pen?*" answer, an "Instrument;" [a *kind* or *species* of Instrument;] "What is a circle?" "A curvilinear-plane-figure:" so also "a Magnet" would be said to be a "Species [or kind] of Iron ore," &c.

When you are asked "What kind of [or "what sort of"] instrument is a pen?" you would answer, One designed *for writing;*" this being what *characterizes* it, and distinguishes it from *other* instruments; "What kind of animal is Man?" the answer will be " Rational;" as distinguishing the Species from other animals; "What kind of plane-curvilinear-figure is a circle?" answer "One whose circumference is everywhere equidistant from the Centre;" which circumstance distinguishes it from an Ellipse: &c.

Such a Predicable then is technically called the "*Difference;*" [or by the Latin name "Differentia;"] in popular language, frequently, the "Characteristic," or the "distinguishing point." And the " Difference" together with the " Genus," are technically spoken of as "*constituting* ["making-up"] the "Species."

Any quality [or "attribute"] which *invariably and peculiarly* belongs to a certain Species, but which yet is not that which we fix on as characterizing the Species, is technically called a "*Property*" [or "Proprium"] of that Species. Thus "risibility" [or the faculty of laughter] is reckoned a " Property" of Man: one of the " Properties" of a Circle is, that any angle drawn in a semicircle is a right-angle: &c.

The power of "attracting iron" might be taken as the "difference [or "characteristic"] of a Magnet; and its "Polarity" as a " Property:" or again, this latter might be taken as its Difference, and the other reckoned among its Properties.

For it is evidently a mere question of convenience, *which* in any such case we fix on as the Characteristic of the Species we are contemplating. And either the one arrangement, or the other, may be the more suitable, according to the kind of pursuit we may be engaged in.

An Agriculturist, for instance, (see Lesson VIII. § 5), would not characterize each kind of plants in the same way as a Botanist, or again, as a Florist; no more would a Builder and a Geologist, and a Chemist, characterize in the same way the several kinds of stones.

§ 3. Any Predicable which belongs to *some* (and not to other) individuals of the same Species, [or which "may be present or absent, the Species remaining the same,"] is called an "*Accident.*"

And these are of two kinds. A "Separable-accident" is one which may be *removed from the Individual;* [or, which may be absent or present, in that which we regard as one and the same individual;] as, for instance (in an example formerly given), the "Sun" is regarded as the same individual thing, whether "rising," or "setting" or in any other situation relatively to the spot we are in: "rising," therefore, or, "setting" are separable accidents of the Sun.

So also, to be in this or that *dress* or *posture*, would be a separable-accident of an individual man; but to be a *native of France*, or of England, or to be of a certain *character*, would be "inseparable-accidents."

It is by inseparable accidents that we commonly distinguish one Individual from another of the same Species, and to enumerate such accidents is called "giving *Description.*" (See below, § 10.)

Of course it is only from *individuals* that any "Accident" can be "inseparable;" for anything that is inseparable from a Species, [or, which forms a part of the signification of a Term by which we denote a certain Species,] is not an Accident, but a Property.

§ 4. Some writers enumerate among Properties such Predicables as are *peculiar* but not *universal;* that is, which do not apply each to *every* individual of a certain species, but are *peculiar* to that species, as *Man alone* can be "virtuous,"—can be a "philosopher," &c., which are attributes not belonging to man. But these are more correctly reckoned Accidents, though Accidents *peculiar* to the Species.

Some again speak of "Properties" which are *universal* but *not peculiar;* as "to breathe air" belongs to the *whole* human species, but not to that species *alone.* Such a Predicable however is not, strictly speaking, a Property of the *Species* "Man," but a property of a higher [more *comprehensive*] Species, "land-animal;" which stands in the relation of "*Genus*" to the species "Man." And it would be called accordingly, in the language of some writers, a "*generic*-property of Man." A Property, strictly so called, of any Species under our consideration, would be called its "*specific*-property."

Predicables then have been usually divided into these five heads: "Genus, Species, Difference, Property, and Accident."

You are to remember, that as every Predicable is so called *in relation to* the Terms of which it can be (affirmatively) predicated, so, each Common-term is to be regarded as belonging to this or that Head of Predicables, according to the Term to which it is in each instance applied, or which may be applied to it. Thus the term "Iron-ore" is a *Species* in respect of the term "Mineral," and a *Genus* in respect of the term "Magnet;" and so in other instances.

§ 5. When we "enumerate *distinctly*" [or "separately"] the several things that are signified by one Common-term, —as the several Species included under some Genus—we are said to "*divide*" that Common-term. Thus, "natural-productions" are *divided* into "Animal, Vegetable, and Mineral;" and each of these again may be subdivided into several "members;" and so on.

Perhaps the word "*distinguish*," if it had been originally adopted, would have been preferable to "*divide*;" (which, however, has been so long in general use in this sense, that it could not now be changed;) because "*Division*" being (in this sense) a *metaphorical* word, the "*Division*" we are now speaking of is liable to be confounded with "Division" in the other (which is the original and proper) sense of the word.

"Division," in its primary sense, means separating from each other (either actually, or in enumeration) the parts of which some really-existing single object consists: as when you divide "an animal" (that is, any single animal) into its several members; or again, into its "bones, muscles, nerves, blood-vessels," &c. And so, with any single Vegetable, &c.

Now each of these *parts* into which you thus "physically" (as it is called) divide "an animal," is strictly and properly a "part," and is *really* less than the whole; for you could not say of a bone, for instance, or of a limb, that it is "an Animal."

In the very same sense, we divide any *Group* ["Class"] of objects, by separating (actually or mentally) those objects from each other; as, when all the Cattle on a farm are divided into cows, horses, sheep, &c., or again, when the horses are divided, that is, placed separate from each other. Each horse is, here, actually less than "all the horses;" and again, all the horses, less than "all the Cattle." But we commonly designate each Group [or Class] by a term that is applicable not merely to the whole Class collectively, but to each one of the objects thus placed together: as, for instance, the term "Metal" may be applied not only to all the Metal that exists, but to any kind of Metal, and to any portion of each kind; and so also "Iron" may be applied not only to all the Iron existing, but to any individual piece of Iron.

And hence men have been led to employ the word "divide" metaphorically, (as has been said above,) in reference to the term itself which denotes a Class; as, when we speak of dividing "Metal"—that is the *Genus* "Metal"—into Gold, Silver, Iron, &c., or "Animal"— that is, the *Genus* "Animal"—into Beast, Bird, Fish, &c.

Now when you thus—in the secondary sense of the word —"divide" a Genus,—that is, the term denoting a Genus, —each of the *parts* [or "members"] is metaphorically called a "part," and is, in another sense, *more* than the whole [the Genus] that is thus divided. For you may say of a Beast or Bird that it is an "Animal;" and the term "Beast" implies not only the term "Animal" but something more besides; namely, whatever "Difference" *characterizes* "Beast" and separates it from "Bird," "Fish," &c.

And so also any Singular-term [denoting one individual] implies not only the whole of what is understood by the Species it belongs to, but also more; namely, whatever distinguishes that single object from others of the same Species: as "London" implies all that is denoted by the term "City" and also its distinct existence as an individual city.

§ 6. The "parts" ["members"] in that figurative sense with which we are now occupied, are each of them *less than the whole*, in another sense; that is, of *less comprehensive* signification. Thus the Singular-term "Romulus" embracing only an individual king, is *less extensive* than the Species "King;" and. that, again, less extensive than the Genus "Magistrate," &c.

An "*Individual*" then is so called from its being *incapable of being* (in this figurative sense) *divided*.

And though the two senses of the word "Division" are easily distinguishable when explained, it is so commonly employed in each sense, that through inattention, confusion often ensues.

We speak as familiarly of the "division" of "Man" (meaning Mankind) into the several races of "Europeans, Tartars, Hindoos, Negroes," &c., as of the "division" of the Earth into "Europe, Asia, Africa," &c., though "the Earth" [or "the World"] is a singular term, and denotes what we call *one Individual*. And it is plain, we could not say of Europe, for instance, or of Asia, that it is a "World." But we can predicate "Man" of every individual European, Hindoo, &c.

And here observe, that there is a common colloquial incorrectness (increasing the liability to confusion) in the use of the word "division" in each of these cases, to denote *one of the "parts"* into which the whole is divided. Thus you will sometimes hear a person speak of Europe as one "division" of the Earth : or of such and such a "division" of an Army : meaning "*portion*." And so again a person will sometimes speak of "animals that belong to the *feline division* of the Carnivora" [flesh eating animals] meaning that portion of the Class "Carnivora."

§ 7. Division, in the sense in which we are here speaking of it, (the figurative,) is evidently the reverse process to "Generalization." (See Lesson VII. § 4.) For as, in *generalizing*, you proceed by *laying aside the differences* between several things, and *abstracting* that which is *common* to them, so as to denote them,—all and each,—by one Common-term, so, in *dividing*, you proceed by *adding on the differences*, so as to distinguish each by a *separate* term.

When you take any Common-term to be divided and subdivided, for any purpose you have in hand,—as, the Term "Animal" in a work on zoology—that term is called your "*Summum* [highest] *genus*," the several Species into which you proceed to divide it, and which are afterwards divided each into other Species, are called, each of them, a "Subaltern" Species or Genus; being, each, a Species in relation to that which can be predicated of it, and a Genus in relation to the Species of which it can be predicated.

Thus "Iron-ore" (in the example lately given) is a Subaltern Species, or Genus in relation to " Mineral" and to " Magnet" respectively.

Any Species that is "*not* made a Genus of any lower Species," in the division you happen to be engaged in,—or, in other words, which is not regarded as any further *divisible* except into *individuals*,—is usually called (by the Latin name) "*infima* Species;" that is, the "*lowest* Species."

"*Proximum* Genus" is a technical name often used to denote the "*Genus-next-above*" [or " nearest,"] the Species you may be speaking of; as "Iron-ore" would be the "*nearest*" [proximum] *Genus*, of Magnet; and " Mineral" would be its *more remote* Genus ; that is, the Genus of *its* Genus.

§ 8. It is usual, when a long and complex course of Division is to be stated, to draw it out, for the sake of clearness and brevity, in a form like that of a genealogical "*Tree.*" And by carefully examining any specimen of such a "Tree" (going over it repeatedly, and comparing each portion of it with the explanations above given) you will be able perfectly to fix in your mind the technical terms we have been explaining.

Take for instance as a "Summum-Genus" the mathematical term.

" Plane-superficial-figure."

Mixed Figure   Rectilinear Figure   Curvilinear Figure
(of Rect. and Curv.)

Triangle Quadrilateral, &c. Circle Ellipse, &c.

Such a " Tree of division" the student may easily fill up for himself. And the employment of such a form will be found exceedingly useful, in obtaining clear views in any study you are engaged in.

For instance, in the one we have been now occupied with, take for a Summun-Genus, " expression ;" (*i. e.,* " expression-in-language" of any such mental-operation as those formerly noticed ;) you may then exhibit, thus, the division and subdivision of—

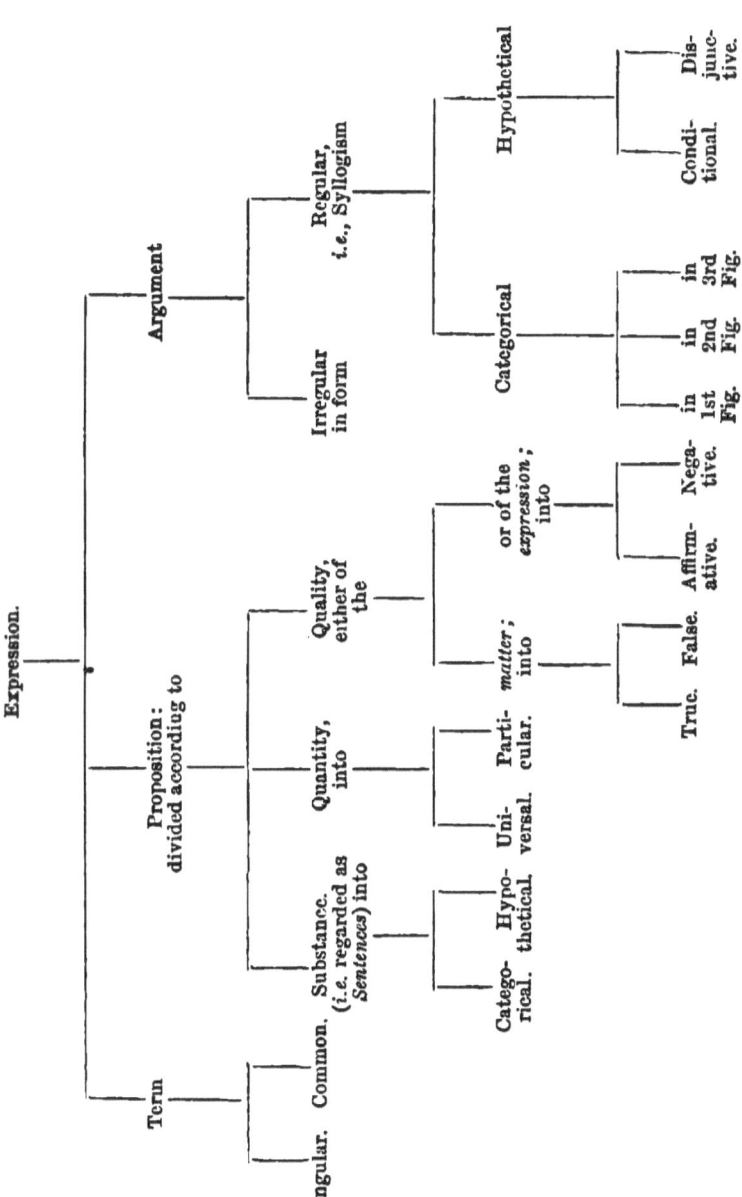

§ 9. The rules for dividing correctly are,

i. That the Whole [or Genus-to-be-divided] be *exactly equal* to all the parts [or Members] together. Nothing therefore must be *included* of which the Genus can *not* be (affirmatively) predicated;—nothing *excluded,* of which it *can.*

ii. The Members [Parts] must be "contradistinguished," (or, as some writers express it, "opposed,") and not *include one another;* which they will do if you mix up together *two or more kinds of division,* made by introducing several *distinct classes of differences.*

Thus, if you were to divide "Books" into "Ancient, Modern, Latin, French, English, Quarto, Octavo, Poems, Histories," &c., (whereof a "modern-book" might be "French," or "English"—a "Poem," or a "History," &c., a "Quarto-book," "ancient" or "modern," &c.,) you would be mixing together four different kinds of divisions of Books; according to their Age, Language, Size, and Subject.

And there are what are called *Cross-divisions;* (because they run *across each other,* like vertical and horizontal sections of anything;) being divisions formed according to "distinct classes of Differences:" or, in other words, "on several distinct *principles* of division."

It is a useful practical rule, whenever you find a discussion of any subject very preplexing and seemingly confused, to examine whether some "Cross-division" has not crept in unobserved. For this is very apt to take place : (though of course such a *glaring* instance as that in the above example could not occur in practice:) and there is no more fruitful source of indistinctness and confusion of thought.

When you have occasion to divide anything in several different ways,—that is, "on several principles-of-division" —you should take care to state distinctly *how many* divisions you are making, and on what principle each proceeds.

For instance, in the "Tree" above given, it is stated, that "Propositions" are divided in different ways, "*according to*" this and that, &c. And thus the perplexity of Cross-division is avoided.

§ 10. iii. A division should not be "*arbitrary;*" that is, its Members should be distinguished from each other by

" Differences" (see above, § 7.) either expressed or readily
understood ; instead of being set apart from each other at
random, or without any sufficient ground.   For instance,
if any one should divide "coins" into "gold-coins," "silver,"
and "copper," the ground of this distinction would be intelligible : but if he should, in proceeding to subdivide
silver coin, distinguish as two branches on the one side,
"shilling," and on the other, "all silver-coins *except* shillings," this would be an *arbitrary* Division.   (See below,
§ 13.)

iv.   A Division should be *clearly arranged* as to its
Members : that is, there should be as much subdivision as
the occasion may require : and not a mere catalogue of the
"lowest-Species," omitting *intermediate* classes [*"subaltern"*]
between these and the " highest-genus :" nor again an in-
termixture of the "subaltern" and "lowest species," so
as to have, in any two branches of the division, Species
contradistinguished and placed opposite, of which the
one ought naturally to be placed *higher up* [near the
" Summum"] and the other *lower down* in the Tree.

For instance, to divide "plane-figure" at once, into
'equilateral triangles, squares, circles, ellipses," &c., or
again "vegetable" into "elms, pear-trees, turnips, mush-
rooms," &c., or again to divide "Animal" into " Birds,
Fishes, Reptiles, Horses, Lions," &c., would be a trans-
gression of this rule.

And observe, that (as was formerly remarked),
although such *glaring* cases as are given by way of
examples could not occur in practice, errors precisely
corresponding to them may and often do occur; and
produce much confusion of thought and error.

§ 11.   When you state the *Genus* that any Species belongs to, together with the Difference that *constitutes* it
["characterizes" it, so as to separate it from the rest],
you are said to give a "*Definition*" of that species.

As " the Magnet," (meaning a *natural*-magnet, is)
defined "an iron ore, having an attraction for iron :" a
" Triangle," a " three-sided figure :" a " Proposition," an
"indicative," [affirming or denying] " Sentence," " Iron-
ore"—" Figure"—" Sentence" are evidently each of the

Genus, in these definitions respectively; and the other part the *Difference*.

This is accounted the most perfect and proper kind of Definition. And the two portions of which it consists— the "Genus" and the "Difference" are called technically the "metaphysical parts:" as not being two real parts into which any individual object can be *actually* divided, but only different views taken [or notions formed] of a Class of objects, by our mind.

What is called a "physical-definition" is made by an enumeration of such parts of some object as are *actually separable;* such as are the Subject, Predicate and Copula of a Proposition; the root, trunk, branches, bark, &c. of a Tree; &c.

A Definition which proceeds by enumerating several *Properties*,—or—in the Case of an Individual—*Inseparable-accidents*, is called a *"Description;"* or, according to some writers, an "Accidental-Definition."

It is evident, that an *Individual* can be defined *only* by a Description; that is, by stating the *Species* and (not *"Properties;"* since *they* belong to *all* the individuals of the Species; but) the *Inseparable•accidents.* As "Alexander

the Great" would be described as "a $\overset{\text{Sp.}}{\overline{\text{King}}}$" . . "of Mace-

don, who subdued Persia ; " "Paris," "The capital . . $\overset{.\,\text{Sp.}}{\overline{\text{City}}}$ . . . of France·"

§ 12. Definitions have also been distinguished—according to the *object designed to be effected* by each—into " Nominal" and " Real."

A Nominal-definition is usually described as being one which explains merely the *meaning of the word* defined ; and a Real-definition, that which explains the *nature of the thing* signified by that word.

Now it may naturally occur to you to ask, are not these (at least in defining a common-term) the same thing? since the object of our thoughts when we employ a Common-term is (see above, Lesson vii. § 7)—not any such *really-existing*-thing as those imaginary abstract-ideas speak of, but,—the *Term* itself, regarded as a "*Sign,*" &c., as was formerly explained.

And in many cases, accordingly, the "Nominal" and the "Real" Definition do coincide. But by a "*Nominal*–definition, is meant (strictly speaking), one which expresses exactly what the *Name* itself conveys to *every-one* who understands that name : and *nothing beyond* this. And any Definition may be called (in a greater or less degree) a *Real*-definition which explains anything—more or less, —*beyond* what is necessarily implied in the Name itself.

Thus, any one who gives such an account of some one of the "metals" for instance, or of the "Sun," as modern researches would enable him to give, would be advancing beyond a mere Nominal-definition; since, in this latter,— the mere explanation of the words "iron" or "sun"—we and our ancestors 500 years ago, would coincide; since both they and we use those words in the same sense; though they knew much less than we do of the nature of those things.

In the case of strictly-*scientific*-terms, the Nominal and the Real-definition may be regarded as coinciding. Thus, the mathematical-definition of a Circle, may be considered as strictly "Nominal," inasmuch as it denotes precisely the same as the *word* "Circle," and nothing beyond ; every name being (in Mathematics) regarded as merely the "definition abridged." And again, it may be regarded as so far a "*Real*-definition," that it conveys all that *can belong* to the thing spoken of, since there can be *no* property of a Circle that is *not* in fact *implied in the definition* of a Circle : or, which is the same thing, in the name, "Circle." It is therefore *as much of a* real-definition as *can* conceiv· ably be given of a Circle.

And so with other scientific-terms. In respect of these, in short, the *meaning of the name*, and the *nature of the thing*, are one and the *same*.

And accordingly, in Mathematics, the definitions are the *Principles* from *which our reasonings set out.*

On the other hand, since a "diamond," or a "planet," or a "sheep," &c., have each of them (that is, each individual of any such Species) a real, actual existence in nature, independently of our thoughts, any of these may possess attributes not implied in the meaning we attach to the

name; and which are to be discovered by observations
and experiments. Any explanation, however, of the nature
of any object *beyond* what is implied in the signification of
its name, is not usually called a "Definition; but the word
"Description" is often used to *denote such* an explanation.

§ 13. What we are concerned with at present is
"Nominal-definition;" it being important with a view to
Reasoning, to ascertain the exact sense in which each
Term is employed, and especially to guard against any
ambiguity in the *Middle*-term of an Argument.

The rules [or cautions] commonly laid down in various
treatises for framing a Definition, are very obvious: namely,

i. That a Definition should be *"adequate;"* i. e., comprehending neither more, nor less, than the term to be
defined.   For instance, if in a definition of "Money" you
should specify its being "made of metal," that would be
too *narrow*, as excluding the *shells* used as money in some
parts of Africa : if again you would define it as an "article
of value given in exchange for something else," that
would be too *wide*, as it would include things exchanged
by *barter ;* as when a shoemaker who wants coals, makes
an exchange with a collier who wants shoes.*

And observe, that such a defect in a Definition cannot
be remedied by making an *arbitrary exception;* (such as
was alluded to above, § 10;) as if for instance and it is
an instance which actually occurred) a person should give
such a Definition of "Capital" as should include (which
he did not mean to do) "Land;" and should then propose
to remedy this by defining "Capital" any "property of
such and such a description *except Land.*"

ii. The other caution usually given, is, that a Definition should be *clearer* than the Term defined : clearer,
that is, to *the persons* you are speaking to : since that may
be obscure to one man which is intelligible to another.

And this rule evidently includes (what some give as a
third rule) a caution against excessive prolixity, excessive
brevity, and ambiguous language.

---

* See Lesson I. on *Money Matters.*

PART IV.

FALLACIES.

LESSON XVI.

§ 1. Although sundry kinds of Fallacies have been from time to time noticed in the forgoing Lessons, it will be worth while to make some further observations thereon.

By a "Fallacy" is commonly meant "any *deceptive* argument or apparent argument, whereby a man is himself convinced—or endeavours to convince others—of something which is not really proved."

Fallacies have been usually divided into two Classes; those in the *form,* and those in the *matter :* though the difference has not been in general clearly explained.

The clearest way of proceeding will be to consider a "Fallacy-in-form" as one in which the Conclusion does not really *follow* from the Premises; and a "Fallacy-in-matter" as one where the Conclusion does follow from the Premises, though there will be still something faulty in the procedure.

In this latter case (where the Conclusion does follow) one may either object to the *Premises* as being "unduly-assumed," or to the *Conclusion* as *irrelevant ;* that is, different, in some way, from what *ought* to have been proved—namely, from what was originally maintained,—from what had been undertaken to be established,—from what the particular occasion requires ; &c.

These that have been mentioned (as the "Fallacies-in-form," and "in matter") must evidently include *every possible* Fallacy ; since whatever objection can be brought against any argument, or apparent argument, must be an objection either against the *Conclusion,* or against the *Premises,* or against the *connexion between* the premises and conclusion ; that is, against the *conclusiveness* of the apparent argument.

§ 2. "Fallacies-in-form," [in which the Conclusion does not really follow from the Premises] are such as we have already given examples of, as violations of the rules above-explained : such as "undistributed-middle,"—"illicit-process," &c.

Among others was noticed the fault of an "*equivocal* Middle-term," taken in one sense in the one premise, and in a different sense in the other. And since this Fallacy turns on the *meaning of words*, and not on the mere form in which the argument is expressed, some may be disposed to rank it rather under the Head of " Fallacies-in-matter."

The most convenient course, however, will be to keep to the-division already laid down; and, accordingly, to reckon the Fallacy of "equivocal-middle" along with all the others in which the conclusion *does not follow* from the Premises.

And, in truth, the technical rules do apply to this—the "Fallacy of equivocation"—*as soon as* it is ascertained that the Middle-term *is* employed in two different senses, and consequently is, in reality, not one, but *two* terms.

But of course the rules of Syllogism do not, alone, enable us to ascertain the meaning or meanings of any Term. *That* must be judged of from our knowledge of the subject-matter,—from the *context*, [or general *drift* of the discourse]—and often from what we know or believe concerning the writer or speaker.

And the same may be said, in many cases, in respect of not only the *signification*, but also the *distribution* or non-distribution, of a Term ; on which depend the fallacies of "undistributed-middle" and " illicit-process." For when a Proposition is expressed *indefinitely* (as " Man invents arts ;" " Man is mortal ;") we are left to judge from the subject-matter, &c., whether it is to be understood as Universal or as Particular.

And again, the sign "all," (which in an Affirmative-proposition, denotes Universality) in a Negative-proposition, *generally*, though *not invariably*, indicates a *Particular ;* that is, usually, though not always, the negation is understood as a *negation of universality*. For instance, of these two propositions, " all they that trust in Him shall not be confounded," and " we shall not all sleep," the one would be understood as Universal, and the other, as Particular.

Observe also that the sign "all" is sometimes understood as meaning "all-*collectively ;*" sometimes "every-one, *separately.*" As "*all* the apples on that tree are enough to fill a bushel ;" i.e., all *together;* and " they are *all* ripe ;" i. e., *every one.*

If this ambiguity be overlooked, two propositions, both true, may appear to be Contradictories. For instance, "All these apples are worth twenty shillings ;" and " Some of these apples are not worth twenty shillings." The right contradictory would be "All these apples together are not worth twenty shillings."

There is an ambiguity answering to this, in the word "some," which ocasionally means "some definite one," and occasionally, "*either* one or *else* another." For instance, if I say "some food is vegetable," I mean that "there actually exists some kind of vegetable food ;" and this being true, its contradictory, "no food is vegetable," must be false. But if I say "some food is necessary to life," the *apparent* contradictory, "no food is necessary to life," is, in a certain sense, true ; for there is no one definite article of food of which it can be said that it is necessary to life. But *some article of food or other* is necessary; which is the meaning of the original proposition ; and the real contradictory to it will therefore be, "all food is *not necessary* to life ;" i. e., " life may be supported without any food at all." [See § 12 of this Lesson.]

§ 3. You are to observe that we cannot always decide absolutely as to *which* Class we should pronounce some particular fallacy to fall under, those in "form" or those in "matter:" because it will often happen, when an argument is stated (which is usually the case) as an *Enthymeme*, that the *suppressed* premise may be *either* one which is *false*, but which *would*, if granted, make the Syllogism complete: or else one which is *true*, but which would *not* complete a regular Syllogism. Now, on the former supposition, the Fallacy would be in the "*matter;*" on the other supposition, it would be in the "*form.*"

For instance, in this Enthymeme, "The Country is distressed ; therefore it is misgoverned," we cannot decide absolutely whether the premise meant to be understood, is, "every Country that is distressed is misgoverned ;" which would make the *syllogism* correct, but would not be admitted as true; or, every Country that is misgoverned is distressed; which would leave the Middle-term undistributed.

And again, when both Premises are expressed, it will often happen (as in an example formerly given) that we have the *alternative* of *either* denying the *truth* of one of the premises,—supposing the Middle-term used in the *same* sense in both—or denying the *conclusiveness* of the argument, supposing the Middle-term used in *each premise* in such a *sense as to make that premise true*. If by "*contrary to experience*" you mean *two different* things, in the two premises, respectively, then, each is, by itself, true, but they prove nothing: if you mean by it the *same* in both premises, respectively, then, one of them is untrue.

§ 4. But observe, that when you mean to charge any argument with the fault of "equivocal-middle," it is not enough to say that the Middle-term is a word or phrase which *admits* of more than one meaning; (for there are few that do not;) but you must show, that, in order for each premise to be admitted, the Term in question must be understood in one sense (pointing out *what* that sense is) in one of the premises, and, in another sense, in the other.

And if any one speaks contemptuously of "over-exactness" in fixing the precise sense in which some term is used,—of attending to minute and subtle distinctions, &c., you may reply that these *minute* distinctions are exactly those which call for careful attention; since it is *only* through the neglect of *these* that Fallacies ever escape detection.

For a very *glaring* and palpable equivocation could never mislead any one. To argue that "feathers dispel darkness, because they are *light*," or that "this man is agreeable, because he is *riding*, and *riding* is agreeable," is an equivocation which could never be employed but in jest. And yet, however slight in any case may be the distinction between the two senses of a Middle-term in the two premises, the apparent-argument will be equally inconclusive; though its fallaciousness will be more likely to escape notice.

Even so, it is for want of attention to *minute* points that houses are robbed, or set on fire. Burglars do not in general come and batter-down the front door; but climb in at some window whose fastenings have been neglected.

And an incendiary, or a careless servant, does not kindle a tar-barrel in the middle of a room, but leaves a lighted turf, or a candle-snuff, in the thatch, or in a heap of shavings. In many cases, it is a good maxim, to " take care of little things, and great ones will take care of themselves."

§ 5. Of the Fallacies of "undistributed-middle" and of " illicit-process," &c., (which have been formerly explained,) no more need be said in this place.

But in respect to the " Fallacy of equivocation," it is worth while tb notice briefly some of the different modes in which a word or phrase comes to be employed in several senses.

i. That may be reckoned an *accidental* equivocation, in which there is no *perceived* connexion between the different senses. Thus "pen " is an instrument for writing, or an enclosure for cattle; "turtle" a kind of bird, and a kind of tortoise ; and "case " is used (as was noticed in Lesson VII. § 3) in three senses. Of this kind is the ambiguity of several proper-names (as John, Thomas, &c.) also notified in the same place.

ii. There are several words which are ambiguous from being employed in what is technically called a "*first-intention*" and a "*second-intention.*"

A "second-intention," of any word is that signification which it bears in reference to some particular art, science, study, pursuit, or system: and its first-intention is its ordinary colloquial sense when there is no such reference.

Thus the ordinary signification of the words "ship," "beast," and " bird," every one knows; but sailors *limit* the word "ship" to vessels of a certain construction ; "beast" is the word applied by farmers in some parts, especially and exclusively, to the "*ox*-tribe;" and " bird" is used in a " second-intention" by sportsmen, to signify " partridge."

§ 6. It is evident, that a word may have several different " Second-intentions," according to the several systems &c. into which it may be introduced as one of the technical-terms.

Thus, "line" is technically employed in Geometry, in Geography, in the Military-art, in the Art of Angling, in Printing, &c.

F

The word "*Species*" is employed by *Naturalists* in a certain "Second-intention" when they are speaking of organized-beings.

The ordinary sense ["first intention"] of the word, is that which has been explained in these Lessons; but Naturalists restrict it to such a class of animals or plants as are supposed to have *descended from a common Stock*.

In ordinary discourse, any one would say that a "Grey-hound" or a' "Mastiff" is a kind ["Species"] of dog; but a Zoologist would say (in technical language) that these are only "*Varieties*," and that all dogs are of one *Species*. So also, in common discourse, any one would speak of "Cauli-flower," and several others, as "kinds" of "Cabbage:" but the Botanist reckons all these as "varieties" of the single Species, Cabbage.

Those, in short, which are (in the technical language of these Lessons) the "lowest-species" that the Naturalist treats of, are called by him, not Species, but *Varieties;* and, again, those classes *under* which his Species come, he never calls *Species* of a higher Genus, but *Genera, Orders,* &c.

Much confusion of thought has often arisen from over-looking this technical-sense ["second-intention"] of the word "Species."

In some instances, the "second-intention" [or philosophical sense] of a word is,—instead of being more *limited*, —more *extensive* than the "first-intention" [or popular sense].

Thus "affection," which is limited, in popular use, to "love," is employed by philosophers as comprehending both "benevolent and malevolent affections." So also "charity," which is often, in popular use, confined to "almsgiving"—"flower," to such flowers as have conspicuous petals,—and "fruit," to such fruits as are "eatable," have each a technical second-intention, which is more extensive.

§ 7. iii. A word will often be employed to denote (in different senses) two things which have a "*resemblance*," or an "*analogy*" to each other.

A "blade" of *grass*, or of a *sword*, have the same name from the direct resemblance between the things themselves.

But instances of this kind are far less common than those in which the same name is applied to two things, not from their being *themselves* similar, but from their having *similar relations* to certain other things. And this is what is called "Analogy."

Thus, the sweetness of a "sound" and of a "taste" can have no *resemblance;* but the word is applied to both, by *analogy,* because as a "sweet" taste *gratifies* the palate, so does a "sweet" sound the ear.

Thus also we speak in the "secondary" [or "transferred," or "analogical"] sense of the "hands" of a Clock,—the "legs" of a Table,—the "foot" of a Mountain,—the "mouth" of a River, &c.; which words in their "primary" ["proper," or original] sense, denote the "hands" of a man,—the "legs, foot, and mouth" of animals; from the *similar relations* in which they stand to other things respectively, in reference to use, position, action, &c.

The words pertaining to *Mind* may in general be traced up, as borrowed, (which no doubt they all were, originally) by Analogy, from those pertaining to *Matter:* though in many cases the primary sense has become obsolete.

Thus "edify,"* in its primary sense of "build up,"† is disused, and the origin of it often forgotten; although the substantive "edifice" remains in common use in a corresponding sense.

When, however, we speak of "weighing" the reasons on both sides,—of "seeing" or "feeling" the force of an argument,—"imprinting" anything on the memory, &c., we are aware of these words being used analogically.

It is in an analogical sense that "Division," "Part," and several other technical terms, have been employed in these Lessons.

§ 8. There are two kinds of error—each very common —which lead to confusion of thought in our use of ana-logical words:

i. The error of supposing the *things themselves* to be similar, from their having *similar relations* to other things.

ii. The still commoner error of supposing the Analogy to *extend* further than it does; [or, to be more *complete*

---

* See 1 Peter ii. 5.   †. See JOHNSON'S *Dictionary.*

than it really is;] from not considering *in what* the Analogy in each case consists.

For instance, the "*Servants*" that we read of in the Bible, and in other translations of ancient books, are so called by Analogy to servants among us: and that Analogy consists in the offices which a "servant" performs in waiting on his master, and doing his bidding. It is in this respect that the one description of "servant" "corresponds" ["answers"] to the other. And hence some persons have been led to apply all that is said in Scripture respecting Masters and *Servants*, to these times, and this country: forgetting that the Analogy is not *complete*, and extends no further than the point above mentioned. For the ancient "servants" (except when expressly spoken of as *hired*-servants) were *Slaves;* a part of the Master's *possessions*.

§ 9. iv. A word will often (in different senses) be applied to two things, connected, not by Resemblance or Analogy, but by the circumstances of *time or place*, as being "Cause and Effect," or "Part and Whole," &c.

Thus, when we say "wormwood has a bitter *taste*," and "I have a bitter *taste* in my mouth," it is plain that the "taste" of wormwood is not a *sensation* in wormwood, (as our taste is in us,) and cannot resemble or be analogous to a sensation; but is the *cause* of the "sensation" of "taste" in me.

This kind of transfer of a word from its "primary" to a "secondary" sense, is called "*Metonymy*." It is thus we speak of a "Crown," or a "Throne," for "regal-power," "the sword," for "war;" a "voice" for a "declaration;" and a man is said to be "*worth*" such and such a sum of money; meaning that he *possesses property that is worth* so much, &c.

Much confusion of thought, and many Fallacies, have arisen from inattention to this source of ambiguity.* It seems strange, but it is quite true, that things have often been in this way confounded together which have not the least Resemblance or Analogy to each other.

---

* The ambiguity of the word "Division," when used to signify one of the *portions* into which anything is divided (see Lesson XV. § 6) is of this kind.

A remarkable instance of this is to be found in the "primary" and "secondary" uses of such words as "*same*" —"*one*"—"*identical*," &c. In the primary sense they imply "*numerical unity*" [individuality], and do *not* imply, necessarily, any *similarity*. For when we say of any grown man, that he is the "*same* person" whom we remember to have seen when an infant, that is not from his now *resembling* an infant. *Another* infant, now, would be much more like what he then was.

In the "secondary" sense, on the other hand, these words imply *nothing but* exact—or nearly exact—*similarity*. For instance, if a man finds in a mine some metal which turns out to be gold with a small alloy of copper, he would say, it is the *same* metal of which coins, or of which watches are made; or if he finds a stone which proves to be a diamond or ruby exactly such as he had seen in a certain ring, he would say, it is the *same* precious-stone as the one in that ring; not meaning, of course, that—in the strict sense—"one and the same" metal or stone can be in two places at once; but only that there is a perfect similarity.

So, also, several persons are said to be in *one and the same* posture, when they are all *placed alike;* and to have "one and the same" *idea* in their minds, when they are all thinking alike. (See Lesson VII. § 8).

§ 10. Now the mode in which these words have been thus transferred (to the utter bewilderment of the inattentive) is this : *one single* word,—such as "gold," or "man," or "triangle," or "fever,"—will equally well apply to any one piece of gold, or individual man, or triangle, or fever, &c. And so, also, will *one* single *Definition* [or Description] of a triangle : and hence the things themselves come to be called "*one*,"—the "*same*" "*identical*," &c., because all the individuals thus named or described, are (according to the modern phrase, which is very correct) "of the *same description*."

In the transferred [secondary] sense, accordingly, you may observe, that things are often spoken of as "very *nearly* the same, but not *quite;*" there being some small difference between them. In the "primary" sense, on the other hand, "unity"—"identity," &c., do not admit of *degrees*. For instance, "This man," either *is* or *is not* the same person whom I saw formerly when he was an infant or child ; and that, whether he differ much or little, from what he then was.

But what helps to introduce confusion is, that "identity" in the primary sense, is in many cases *judged* of, and "*inferred*," from similarity. For instance, a man may be ready to swear to some picture as *the one* which he had lost, *from* his perceiving a perfect similarity ; and yet it might perhaps be afterwards proved to his satisfaction, that it was *not* that *one*, but an exact copy.

§ 11. Besides the causes of ambiguity that have been just mentioned, it is to be observed that there are several words which it is customary to employ *elliptically;* that is, in *combination* with something *understood;* and that men are apt to forget *when* it is that such a word is used with, and when without, this ellipsis.

For instance, we speak of such a one *possessing* 10,000 *pounds;* (though perhaps he may not *actually* possess ten pounds in money); meaning, that his whole property *would exchange for* that sum. And ordinarily, such a mode of speaking leads to no practical inconvenience. But there is no doubt that it has contributed to foster that enormous practical error known, among Political Economists,* as the "Mercantile System."

So also we speak commonly of "the *example* of such a one's punishment serving to *deter* others from crime." And usually, no misapprehension results from this, which is, in truth, an *elliptical* expression. But sometimes sophistical reasoners take advantage of it, and men who are not clear-headed are led into confusion of thought. Strictly speaking, what deters a man from crime, in such cases as those alluded to, is the *apprehension* of *himself* suffering punishment. *That apprehension* may be excited by the *example* of another's being punished ; or it may be excited *without* that example, if punishment be denounced, and there is good reason to expect that the threat will not be an empty one. And on the other hand, the example of others suffering punishment does not deter any one, if it *fail* to excite this apprehension for himself; if, for

---

* See SENIOR'S and WHATELY'S *Lectures on Political Economy.*

instance, he considers himself as an *exempt* person, as is the case with a despot in barbarian countries, or with a madman who expects to be acquitted on the plea of insanity.

So, also, when any one speaks of being in distress from being "out of work" and of his "seeking for *employment*," we understand him to mean "work by which he can *earn* a *subsistence*." But great errors have often been committed by writers who have lost sight of the elliptical character of the expression, till they have practically forgotten in their reasonings that the thing really desired is, not the *labour* but the *gain*.

To this head may, perhaps, be referred the ambiguity (which has been a source of endless confusion) formerly noticed (Lesson II.) of such words as "because," &c., and again "therefore," and several others.

When, in *accounting for* the wetness which I perceive on the ground, I say, "the ground is wet *because* it has rained, I mean (speaking at full length) to assign the "rain" as the "cause of the *wetness*:" when, again, I *infer* that "it has rained *because* the ground is wet," the meaning of the word "because" is, if fully expressed, that I assign the wetness as the "cause of my *belief*."

The same may be said of such words as "may," "possible," &c., and again, "must," "necessary," &c. (See Lesson X. § 8).

When I say of a man forcibly carried off by enemies, "he *must* go wherever they conduct him," I mean, "*he* cannot avoid *going*:" when I say that on his release "he *must* eagerly return to his home," I mean that "*I* cannot avoid *drawing that conclusion*."

So, also, if I say of a man in health and at liberty, "he *may* go out or stay within," I mean that neither going nor staying is *unavoidable* to *him*: but when I say of a man who is sick, that "he *may* recover," I do not mean (as in the former case) that "this depends on *his choice*," but that "I am not led *unavoidably* to the *conclusion*, that he will recover, or that he will not recover."

§ 12. There are also other ways in which a Term may be so modified in its sense as not to have precisely the same meaning in both premises.

For you are to remember that even any one word which is not itself one of the terms, but only a small portion of one of them, may be so understood as to affect the sense of the whole Term. Even a difference in the *position* of a word in respect of the rest, may greatly alter the sense.

For instance, "He who believes his opinion always right deems himself infallible : you always believe your opinion right; therefore you deem yourself infallible." Here, the premises are both true ; for any opinion which you did *not* believe to be right, would plainly not be *your* opinion ; and it would be difficult to deny that a man considers himself infallible, who should believe that his opinion is invariably right. But the different situation of the word "always" gives a different sense to the Middle-term in the two premises. To " think your opinion always right," means, to have a *general* conviction respecting the *whole of your opinions collectively*, that none of them is ever wrong ; but "always to think your opinion right," means, " to have a *particular* conviction, on each occasion, *separately*, that your opinion on that occasion is right."

A Fallacy of this character—that is, where the Middle-term is taken *collectively* in one premise, and *dividedly* in the other,—is technically called the "Fallacy-of-*division*," or of " *composition;*" according as the Middle-term is understood in a *collective-sense* in the *Major*-premise, and in a *divided sense* in the Minor; or vice versâ.

A glaring example would be, " *all* the apples from that tree are worth 20*s.*; this is an apple from that tree ; therefore it is worth 20*s.*"

Such a fallacy has helped to give plausibility to what has been called " the doctrine of *necessity.*" For instance, " He who necessarily goes or stays" (in reality, " who necessarily goes, or again, who necessarily stays") is not a free-agent; you necessarily go or stay; (that is,— taking these two things *in connexion*,—you " necessarily take the alternative ;") " therefore you are not a free-agent."

§ 13. The way in which this Fallacy usually occurs in practice, is, when something is proved *separately* concerning each one of several things belonging to some class; and then this is considered as having been proved concerning the whole class *collectively;* that is, concerning those things taken in *connexion with each other.*

A man, for instance, swallows a certain drug, and is seized with alarming symptoms; you show that these symptoms may possibly have arisen from other causes; the same drug is swallowed by another man, who is seized with like symptoms; and you show that other causes may have produced the symptoms in him; the same may be shown, suppose, in each separate case (considered each by itself) out of 100; and then you assume that it has been proved that all the men who have taken the drug and exhibited like symptoms may have been affected, all of them, by natural causes.

This kind of argument has been employed to refute the accounts given by the Evangelists of the miracles they record; that is, explaining *some one* of the recorded cures —*considered by itself,* as an accident; and then the same with another, and another; and so on.

Sometimes again a Middle-term is ambiguous from being understood in one premise in *conjunction with certain circumstances* actually pertaining to it, at a particular time, &c., and in the other premise, *independently* of those circumstances. A glaring example would be, if any one should pretend to prove (which of course would be only as a jest) that because what you have on your back was the covering of a sheep, therefore the sheep wore a coat of blue or red broadcloth. This is called in the technical language of the Latin treatises " Fallacia accidentis "

It is evident that when any ambiguity, of whatever kind, in a Middle-term, is suspected, the natural course is to seek for, or to demand, a *Definition* of it. Only, remember that it would be impertinent to insist, in every such case, on a *complete* definition, beyond what is requisite for removing any *doubt as to the argument before us;* i. e. as to the Middle-term's being employed in the same sense in both premises.

For instance, if there were a discussion respecting a person's having *swallowed "poison"* and some ambiguity connected with the reasoning, were suspected in the employment of the word, it would not be necessary to give a definition such as should extend to "*every* poison," including such as savages use for their *arrows:* because the supposed question relates only to poisons taken into the stomach.

§ 14. The Fallacies-in-matter are divided (as has been said) into two kinds: "*undue-assumption-of-a-premise,*" and "*irrelevant conclusion.*"

It is to be observed that no one is to be charged with *fallacious*-proceeding merely because he argues from Premises which we deny; or because the Conclusion he draws is not the one we would wish to see proved. For neither of these implies any *deception.*

One man may assume facts or principles which another will not admit; but provided he does this openly and knowingly, there is no Fallacy in the case.

Or again, we may, (suppose) wish to have it pointed out and proved *who* is the perpetrator of such and such a crime; but if the accused party prove that it was not *he,* we have no right to demand more.

But if any one is convinced by an argument based on some Premise which he would *not* have admitted if *distinctly put before him,* there is in this case a Fallacy.

And so there is, if any one is satisfied, or endeavours to satisfy others, by proving some conclusion, different from what he had *originally maintained;* or from what was originally proposed as the Question: or, (which comes to the same,) which is the contradictory, not, of what he had *originally denied,* but of some different proposition. *This* is properly the Fallacy of "irrelevant conclusion."

§ 15. Under the former of these two classes of Fallacy comes what is, technically, called "begging the Question;" that is, assuming as a Premise the very proposition which —in other words—is proved as the Conclusion. The way in which this is usually done is that which is commonly called, "arguing in a Circle;" that is, proving some conclusion by means of a Premise which is itself deduced—more or less remotely—from premises deduced from that very Conclusion, assumed as a premise. As if you were to prove that A is B, because C is D; and that C is D, because E is F; and so on, till at length you come to infer that Y is Z *because A is* B.

Of course the *narrower* the Circle, the less likely it is to escape the detection, either of the reasoner himself, (for men often deceive *themselves* in this way,) or of his hearers. When there is a long circuit of many intervening proposi-tions before you come back to the original Conclusion, it will often not be perceived that the arguments really do proceed in a "Circle." Just as when any one is advancing in a *straight line* (as we are accustomed to call it) along a plane on this Earth's surface, it escapes our notice that we are really moving along the *circumference of a Circle*, (since the earth is a globe,) and that if we could go on without interruption in the same line, we should at length arrive at the very spot we set out from. But this we readily perceive, when we are walking round a small hill.

For instance, if any one argues that you ought to submit to the guidance of himself, or his leader, or his party, &c., because these maintain what is right; and then argues that what is so maintained is right because it is maintained by persons whom you ought to submit to; and that these are himself and his party; or again, if any one maintains that so and so must be a thing morally wrong, because it is prohibited in the *moral portion* of the Mosaic-law, and then, that the prohibition of it does form a part of the *moral* (not the ceremonial, or the civil) portion of that Law, *because* it is a thing *morally wrong*,—either of these would be too narrow a Circle to escape detection, unless several intermediate steps were interposed. And if the *form of expression* of each proposition be *varied* every time it recurs,—the sense of it remaining the same—this will' greatly aid the deception.

Of course, the way to oppose the Fallacy, is to reverse this procedure: to narrow the Circle by cutting off the intermediate steps: and to exhibit the same proposition,— when it comes round the second time,—in the same words.

§ 16. In all cases,.an *unduly-assumed* premise, (i. e. one which would not be admitted if clearly stated, and delibe-rately considered,) is the more likely to escape detection, the *longer* the train of argument is, and the greater the number of well-established propositions introduced.— When this artifice is employed, a dull or thoughtless hearer is apt to say "there is *much truth* in what has been urged."

And so perhaps there is. There may have been introduced, in the course of the reasoning, twenty propositions,
all of them true, *except one;* the denial of which one would
nullify the whole train of arguments. A chain which
has *only one* faulty link, is not indeed the stronger, but
is the more likely to *appear* strong, by the addition of a
great many sound links

It also contributes to this kind of deception, to *suppress*
the unduly-assumed premise; stating the argument as
an Enthymeme expressing the *true* premise, and giving
proofs of the truth of that, as if everything turned on the
establishment of *that* premise.

So also, in Fallacies of the other class,—the "irrelevant-
conclusion"—it often aids the deception, to *suppress* the
Conclusion itself: bringing forward arguments which do
indeed go to prove *a* Conclusion, somewhat *like* the one
required, though not the very one: and then (instead of
expressly stating the Conclusion that really does follow,
or again, that which had been originally maintained) a
man will say, "the inference from this is plain;" or "I
have thus established my point;" or "the position of our
opponents is thus completely overthrown," &c.

§ 17. The two kinds of "Fallacy-in-matter," are very
commonly combined in one course of argument: that is,
a false or a doubtful premise will be assumed as having
been proved by arguments which go to prove, not *that,*
but another proposition, somewhat like it.

For instance, instead of proving that "this Prisoner has
committed an atrocious fraud," you prove that "the fraud
he is accused of is atrocious:" instead of proving (as in
the well-known tale of Cyrus and the two coats) that "the
taller boy had a right to force the other boy to exchange
coats with him," you prove that "the exchange would
have been advantageous to both;" instead of proving that
"a man has not the right to educate his children, or to
dispose of his property, in the way he thinks best," you
show that the way in which he educates his children, or
disposes of the property, is not really the best; instead of
proving that "the poor ought to be relieved in this way
rather than in that," you prove that the poor ought to be
relieved; instead of proving that "an irrational-agent—

whether a brute or a madman—can never be deterred from any act by apprehension of punishment," (as for instance a dog, from sheep-biting, by fear of being beaten,) you prove that "the beating of one dog does not operate as an *example* to *other* dogs, &c.; and then you proceed to assume as premises, conclusions different from what have really been established.

The chief difficulty in detecting any Fallacy of whatever kind in our own reasonings, or another's, arises (as was formerly remarked) from its being usually stated in an oblique, indirect and somewhat inverted and perplexed form of expression; and more especially when *diluted*, as it were, with a multitude of words; just as poison is more likely to escape detection, when disguised and diluted by being mixed up with a quantity of innocent ingredients, than when presented in a small concentrated dose.

The validity, or the fallaciousness, of any course of reasoning, will then be made the most evident, when examined according to the forgoing rules, after laying aside all redundant words put in for mere embellishment of style, and stating the whole in the most simple language, and in regular order, as briefly as is compatible with perfect clearness.

PART V.

DIFFERENT KINDS OF ARGUMENT.

LESSON XVII.

§ 1. It remains to make a few remarks on the *"finding* [according to the Latin writers, *Invention*] of arguments;" the foregoing Lessons relating only to the rules for *passing judgment* on arguments.

It is to be observed in the first place, that the words *"infer"* and *"prove"* (which we have frequently had occasion to employ,) denote, not *two different things*, but the same thing considered in two *different points of view*. He who "infers" (correctly) *proves;* and he who "proves" infers : and yet the two expressions are not *synonymous*.

So also, the "road from London to Liverpool" and the "road from Liverpool to London," are not different things ; but the one expression calls to the mind the thought of a journey *from* the Metropolis to the Seaport ; and the other, the reverse. And in like manner, the word "infer" fixes the mind *first* on the Premises and then on the Conclusion ; the word "prove," on the contrary, leads the mind *from* the Conclusion (in this case called the "Question") *to* the Premises.

Hence, we say commonly "What do you *infer from* that?" "How do you prove this?" namely, this *Conclusion?*

And the corresponding *Substantives* are often used to denote that which is, in each instance, *last* in the mind : "inference" being often used to signify a *Conclusion* [Proposition-inferred] and "proof," a *Premise*.

When then any long train of reasoning is carried on, we proceed—in "inferring," and in "proving"—in opposite directions : our object being, in the one case, to ascertain from all that we know on a certain subject, *what Conclusion* is to be drawn ; and in another case,—when we are satisfied as to the conclusion—to consider by *what arguments* we shall establish it.

§ 2. In the former case, from established *"data"* [certain known facts, and acknowledged principles] we infer so and so; and from this conclusion, in conjunction with other known truths, we infer something else; and so on, till we have ascertained what is decisive of the question before us, or as much as we are able.

In the latter case, we proceed *upwards* from the Premises which will establish the Conclusion we are maintaining, to the arguments which will prove those Premises: and so on, till we arrive at something that is *admitted*. And from this,—when we have to convince others—we generally proceed through the same train of reasoning, in a reversed order, *downwards*, till we have arrived at the Conclusion to be established.

We are sometimes then employed in what may be called "seeking for a *Conclusion,*" and sometimes again, in "seeking for *Middle-terms.*"

For instance, a *Judge* is inquiring whether the estate does, or does not, belong by law to the claimant: the Suitor (or his Advocate) is seeking for proofs that the estate is his. The Natural-philosopher, when *investigating,* inquires "*what* is the cause of the tides;" the Physician "what is this patient's disease;" and each, when he has satisfied himself, and is proceeding to teach and to convince others, sets himself,—like the Advocate—to seek for *proofs:* sometimes employing the same that had led *himself* to the conclusion, and sometimes different ones; according to what he judges will serve best to satisfy the understanding of others, that "the cause of the tides is so and so;" or that "such and such is the patient's disease."

And thus, in laying before others this process of reasoning, a man will sometimes proceed in the same order in which he had *sought* for the arguments, (that is, beginning from the Conclusion, and proceeding *upwards,*) or again, sometimes in the reverse-order; setting out from something that is admitted, and proceeding *downwards* towards the ultimate Conclusion. *

§ 3. In treating of the operation of seeking for Middle-terms—in other words, for Arguments to establish, on each

---

* See the notice in Lesson IX. of the Analytical and Synthetical order.

occasion, the Conclusion maintained—we are naturally led to inquire concerning the different *kinds* of Arguments one often finds alluded to in books, or in conversation.

These are in general very indistinctly described, and confusedly enumerated.

We hear persons speaking of "Syllogistic Reasoning," and such as is not "Syllogistic;"—of "Categorical, or Hypothetical Arguments,"—or "Demonstrative, and Probable, [or Moral] Reasoning;" of "Direct and Indirect Arguments;"—of "A priori Arguments," "Arguments from Testimony,"—from "Analogy,"—from "Example"—by "Parity-of-Reasoning," &c., without any distinct account being given of these and other modes of procedure.

In reality, to enumerate thus confusedly the several kinds of Argument, is to commit the fault formerly noticed in reference to "cross-divisions;" there being, in this instance, no less than four different divisions; which ought not to be blended together.

First. The division of Arguments into irregular and syllogistic, and of Syllogisms again, into Categorical and Hypothetical, &c., is a division, strictly speaking, not of *Arguments* themselves, but of the *forms of stating* an argument. For it is manifest (as above explained) that one individual argument may be stated in a Hypothetical or in a Categorical form, and in the first Figure, or in the second, &c.

Secondly. The division of Arguments into *probable* and *demonstrative* is evidently according to the *subject-matter:* and is strictly, not a division of *Arguments*, considered *as* arguments, but rather, of the *Propositions* they consist of, in respect of the "matter" of those propositions.

§ 4. *Thirdly.* Arguments are divided into "*direct*" and "*indirect*," according as your object is to establish either the *truth* of the *Conclusion*, or the *falsity* [the "Contradictory"] of one of the *premises*. For when we arrive by sound reasoning, at a false Conclusion, it is plain that one at least of the Premises must be false.

In short, every valid argument may be stated in the form of a *Conditional Proposition;* "*If* the Premises are true, the Conclusion is true;" then, supposing you admit the Premises to be true, you must admit the truth of the

Conclusion; (which corresponds to a *Constructive* Conditional-syllogism;) and hence also, supposing you find the Conclusion false, you must admit that the Premises, or one of them, cannot but be false ; since if they were both true, the Conclusion would be true : and this corresponds to a *Destructive* Conditional-syllogism.

Now the above is evidently a Division, not strictly speaking, of *Arguments*, but of the purposes for which any Argument may be designed : namely, either to prove its Conclusion, or to *dis*prove one its Premises.

For the *same individual Argument* may answer both purposes in different persons. For instance, "Whatever is maintained by the Stoics (or by such and such a philosopher, sect, party, &c.) must be admitted ; that pain is no evil (or such and such a doctrine, whatever it may be, in each instance) is so maintained: therefore this must be admitted :" now a zealous partizan would be so fully convinced of the Premises that he will assent to the Conclusion : others may be so revolted by the Conclusion, that they will thereupon reject the Major-premise.

The Argument therefore will, to the one, be "direct," and to the other "indirect."

§ 5. *Fourthly.* When we speak of arguing from a *Cause* to an Effect, or of arguing from *Testimony* to the truth of what is attested, or again, from a *known case* to an unknown *similar* case, &c., these kinds of arguments are distinguished from each other "according to the *relation existing between the Premises and the Conclusion,* in respect of the *subject-matter* of each."

This then, and this alone, is properly a division of *Arguments, as such.*

When we say, for instance, that in arguing from the "fall of rain" to the consequent "wetness of the roads," the Premise is a *Cause,* and the Conclusion drawn, an *Effect,* it is evident we are not speaking of the more *syllogistic* connexion of the Premise and Conclusion ; (which, as was formerly explained, is always the same ;) nor again are we speaking of the subject-matter of those Propositions (as in the second Head) considered,—each by itself—merely *as* Propositions, independently of the Argument, for "Cause," and "Effect" are *relative* words; and the Premise is called a Cause *of* that Effect which is inferred in the Conclusion. So that it is the *relation*, in respect of *matter*, of the Premise to the Conclusion, that we are speaking of.

And so also in respect of Arguments from Testimony, and the other kinds that have been alluded to.

§ 6. Arguments, then, may be divided, first, into two classes: *First*, such as *might* have been used to *account* for the Conclusion, supposing it had been already granted; and *secondly*, those which could not. Or, in other words, *first*, Arguments from Cause to Effect; and, *secondly*, all other kinds.

For instance, if I infer from a "fall of rain" that "the roads must be wet," I am using an Argument of the former Class [an "A-priori-Argument"]; since if it were *known*, and remarked by any one, that the roads are wet, I should *account* for that fact by informing him that it had rained. Or again, if a person were *known* to have committed a murder, and it were inquired *how he came* to perpetrate such a crime, then, any one would be said to *account* for it, [to show *why* he did it,*] by saying that he was a man of ferocious and revengeful character; or that he was known to bear malice against the deceased; or to have an interest in his death, &c. And these very circumstances might have been used (supposing the charge *not* proved) as an *argument* to cast suspicion on him.

On the other hand, if his guilt were inferred from the *testimony* of some witnesses, or again, from his clothes having been bloody, or from his having about him some property of the deceased, these would be arguments of the other class, since they are such as could not have been employed to *account for* the fact, supposing it established.

§ 7. The Arguments of this latter class may be subdivided into two kinds: which may be called Arguments from "*Sign*," and arguments from "*Example*;" [or, "*Instance*;"] each of which may also be further subdivided.

i. As far as any circumstance is what may be called a "*Condition*,"—more or less necessary—to the existence of a certain effect, phenomenon, event, result, law, &c.—in

---

* It is to be observed, that the word "why" has three different senses: viz. from what *cause?* by what *proofs?* for what *purpose?*

other words, as far as it is a "Condition" of the truth of some assertion or supposition,—so far it (the "condition") may be *inferred* [or "concluded"] from the truth of that assertion or supposition,—from the existence of that effect, &c.

If it be a "Condition" absolutely *essential* to something which we know or assume to be true, it may of course be inferred with complete *certainty;* and the nearer we approach to this case, the stronger will be the probability.

Thus, in the instance just above, when a man is suspected of a murder, from being found near the spot, his clothes bloody, and property of the deceased about him; the perpetration of the murder by him is just so far probable, as it is presumed to be a *Condition* of the existence of the *"Signs;"* i. e. so far as it is presumed that *otherwise* his clothes would *not* have been stained, &c. [or that they would not have been stained *unless* he had committed the deed.]

So also the wetness of the roads is a "Sign" that rain has fallen, just so far as we suppose that *otherwise* the roads would *not* have been wet; in short, that the fall of rain was a *condition* of that wetness.

To this head we may refer all mathematical reasonings. Every property, for instance, of a triangle may be regarded as a "condition" of the supposition that a "Triangle" is what is defined. A figure would *not be* a Triangle, *unless* its angles were equal to right angles, &c.

It is to be observed that although in many Arguments from "Sign"—as when we infer wetness of the roads from a fall of rain—we infer a *Cause* from an *Effect*, this is not *inasmuch* as [or "so far forth as"] it is a *Cause*, but inasmuch as it is a *Condition*. For we should no less infer from finding a certain spot wet, that it had been left *uncovered;* though the mere absence of covering could not be properly called a *Cause* of its wetness.

And in a like manner, a man's having been alive on a certain day, might be inferred as a necessary "Condition" (though certainly not a "Cause") of his dying the next day.

§ 8. *"Testimony"* is one kind of "Sign." For it evidently has weight just so far as we suppose the *truth* of what is attested to be a necessary "Condition" of the testimony; that is, just so far as we suppose that the testimony would *not* have been given, *unless* the thing attested had been true.

The different degrees of weight due to different Testimonies must of course depend on a great variety of circumstances; of which we must, on each occasion, judge in great measure from the particulars of the case then before us.

There are two remarks, however, on this point which are needful to be kept in mind: *first*, we should remember the difference between Testimony to "matters-of-*fact*" and to "matters-of-*opinion*." When the question is about a *fact*, we look, merely or chiefly, to the *honesty* of the witness, and to his *means of obtaining information;* when the question relates to doctrine [or opinion] of any kind, his *ability to judge* must equally be taken into account.

By a "matter [or "question"] of fact," is commonly understood something which might, *conceivably*, be submitted to the *senses;* and about which it is supposed there could be no disagreement between persons who should be present, and to whose senses it should be submitted.

By a "matter of opinion" again, is meant anything whereon an exercise of *judgment* would be called for on the part of persons having the same objects presented to their senses; and who might conceivably disagree in their judgment.

Suppose, for instance, a man is accused of a murder; whether he did or did not strike the blow, or fire the shot, &c. would be a "question of *fact*," whether he did so *wilfully and maliciously* [which is necessary to constitute an act, *murder*] would be a question of ["*judgment*," or] *opinion*.

And observe, that the distinction does not at all turn on the greater or less degree of *certainty* attainable in the two cases respectively. For instance, whether "King Richard the Third, *did*, or *did not* put to death his nephews in the Tower, (which is a "question of *fact*,") is very doubtful, and a matter of dispute among Historians; but *what sort of an act* it was, if he did commit it, is a "matter-of-opinion," but one on which no one would be likely to doubt.

§ 9. In most cases this distinction is very obvious; but it sometimes happens that a person is supposed,—and supposes himself—to be attesting a *fact;* when in truth he is giving an *opinion;* that is, either stating the *inference* he draws *from* the fact he has witnessed; or again, professing to attest a fact which he has not really witnessed, but which he *concludes* to have taken place, from something he did witness.

An instance of the former kind is, when some one who is in attendânce on a sick person bears witness that the patient was benefited, or was disordered, *by* taking such and such a medicine.   He was an eyewitness perhaps, of the medicine's being swallowed, and of the subsequent change, for the better or for the worse; but that the medicine *caused* that change (though he may be very right in believing that it did) is evidently his *judgment.*

As an instance of the other kind, a man, suppose, will attest that he saw such a one killed; though perhaps he did not see him dead; but saw him receive a wound which he *judged* (perhaps very rightly) could not' fail to occasion speedy death.

For it is to be remembered that there may be, and often are "questions-of opinion" *relative* to *facts;* i. e., we *judge* from such and such circumstances, that so and so is, or is not, *likely* to occur; or to exist.   It is a *fact*, that there is, or that there is not, a great lake in the interior of New Holland ; but till that interior shall have been explored, everyone is left to form his opinion, and to judge according to probabilities.

And hence, it should also be remembered, that men are apt to *reason unconsciously;* and thus to suppose themselves bearing testimony (as has been said) to something their senses have witnessed, when in truth they are stating their own inferences therefrom.

The process which usually takes place is this: their senses furnish them with *one Premise*, (the Minor,) the *other* is supplied by their own mind; and the *Conclusion* drawn from these two (as you may see in the above examples) is what they describe themselves as having *witnessed.*

§ 10. ii. The other remark to be borne in mind, is, that when several *independent* witnesses [witnesses between whom there could have been no *collusion*] attest the same thing, the weight of their testimony depends on this *agreement,* and not on the weight of each considered separately, or on the mere *addition* of these together.

Thus, if a stranger, or one on whose veracity I have no reliance, gives me intelligence of some remarkable transaction, or state of things, which he professes to have witnessed, describing fully all the details, I may perhaps think it more likely than not that the whole story and all the particulars are a fabrication. But if I receive the *same* account from another, and again from another person, (equally undeserving of credit,) who could not have had any communication with the first, nor could have had access to any source of false information common to them all, I should at once believe them; because the chances would be immeasurably great against several persons, (however likely, each, to invent *a* story) having independently, invented the *same* story.

And the force of evidence in such an argument depends mainly on the number and minuteness of the *particulars* in the thing attested; because the chances are thus increased against an *accidental* coincidence. ·

The same rule applies not only to "Testimony" but to other "Signs" also. As when, (to refer to an example in the preceding Lesson,) a person after swallowing a certain drug is attacked with such and such symptoms; which may have been accidental; if the same symptoms follow in another case, and another, &c., we are convinced at length that these cannot have been accidental coincidences, but that the drug *caused* the symptoms.

§ 11. When we reason from a known case to another, or others, less known, under the same Class, this is called arguing from "Example"—by "Induction"—from "Experience"—by "Analogy"—by "Parity-of-reasoning," &c., all of which expressions, though not exactly synonymous, denote a process substantially the same. And the two cases,—the known and the unknown,—are said to be *"analogous"* or *"parallel cases;"* the common Class which they both fall under being the point of Resemblance or Analogy between the two.

Thus, we show from the example of the French Revolution, and that of England in the time of Charles the First, that the extreme of Democracy is likely to lead to a military Monarchy.

It is in this sense that we speak of "making an Example" of one who is punished for any faults; so as to deter others by the expectation that a like fault in them will lead to *their* punishment.

And it is thus that we learn to anticipate such and such weather, in certain situations, at certain seasons; and in short, become acquainted with the general *Laws of Nature.*

In all these cases, we proceed, strictly speaking, by Analogy. But this word is most usually employed in those arguments where the correspondence between the two cases is not so complete as to warrant a *certainty* in our conclusions. When the two cases do correspond completely, or nearly so, we usually employ the word *Experience.*

Thus a man would be said to be convinced from "Experience" that such and such a kind of diet, or of medicine, or of weather, is wholesome or unwholesome to himself; if he had invariably observed like effects on a number of men, he might perhaps speak of experience as having convinced him that this diet, &c., was wholesome or unwholesome for the whole human Species; though in this, he would be liable to mistake; but if he conjectured the same with respect to some other Species of animal, every one would say he was reasoning by "Analogy."

§ 12. And here observe, that it is not strictly correct to speak of " Knowing by Experience" such and such a *general truth;* or that so and so *will take place* under such and such circumstances. Not but that we may often have the most complete and rational *assurance* of general truths, or future events; but, properly speaking, what we *know by* "experience," is the *past* only; and those *individual* events which *we* have actually experienced: and any conviction concerning a *general rule* and concerning *future* occurrences, is what we *judge from* Experience.*

And this distinction is important to be remembered, because, although (as we have said) there are numberless cases in which the conclusion thus drawn is not liable to mistake, many persons are apt—as was above remarked—to make mistakes as to *what* it is that they themselves,—or that others,—are, on each occasion, bearing witness to.

A mere fact, or a number of *individual* facts, however strange they may seem to us,—that are attested by a person whose veracity we can fully rely on, we are justified

---

* See the instance formerly cited from Hume, of the argument that "miracles are contrary to experience," &c

in believing, even though he be a man of no superior judgment. But if he states some *general fact* [or "law"] as a thing *experienced* by him, we should remember that this is his *inference, from* his experience. It may be a very correct one: and it may be one in which no great ability is needed for forming a correct judgment; but still the case is one in which his *ability*, as well as *veracity*, is to be taken into account.

For instance, a Farmer or a Gardener will tell you that he "knows by experience" that such and such a crop succeeds best if sown in Autumn, and such a crop again, if sown in Spring. And in most instances they will be right: that is, their Experience will have led them to right *conclusions*. But what they have actually *known by* experience, is, the success or the failure of *certain individual* crops.

And it is remarkable, that for many Ages all Farmers and Gardeners without exception were no less firmly convinced—and convinced of their knowing it by *experience* —that the crops would never turn out good unless the seed were *sown during the increase of the Moon;* a belief which is now completely exploded, except in some remote and unenlightened districts.

§ 13. In all cases, Arguments of the Class we are now speaking of, proceed on the supposition (which is the Major-premise) that "what takes place,—or has happened —or which we are sure *would* happen—in a certain case, must happen, or take place, in a certain other similar [or analogous] case; or in all such cases."

The degrees of probability of this Major-premise will of course be infinitely various, according to the subject-matter. In the investigation of what are called "physical-laws," a single experiment, fairly and carefully made, is often allowed to be conclusive; because we can often *ascertain all the circumstances* connected with the experiment. Thus a Chemist, who should have ascertained by trial, that a specimen of Gold, or of some other metal before him, would combine with Mercury, would at once conclude this to be a property of that metal universally.

In human transactions, on the contrary, it would be thought very rash to draw a conclusion from a single occurrence; or even from two or three. We make, in such cases, a *wide "Induction"* (as it is called) of a number of individual instances, [or "examples,"] before we venture to conclude universally,—or even as a *general* rule—what is likly to be, for instance, the result of such and such a form of Government,—of the existence of Slavery,—of the diffusion of Education,—of Manufactories, &c.

§ 14. We have said that we sometimes argue not only from what has *actually* happened in certain cases, but also from what we feel certain *would* happen in such and such a *supposed* case. Of this description are instructive *"Fables"* [or "Parables," "Apologues," "Illustrations"] in which a general maxim [or "principle"] is inferred from a supposed case, *analogous* to that to which we mean to apply the maxim.

Thus, the imprudence of a man who should hastily join the desciples of Jesus, without having calculated the sacrifices required, and the fortitude expected of him, is illustrated by the supposed case of a man's beginning to build a house without computing the cost.

So also Socrates argued against the practice of some of the Greek republics, who chose their magistrates by *lot*, from the supposed case of mariners casting lots *who* should have the management of the vessel, instead of choosing the best Seaman.

And Nathan's parable brought home to David a sense of the enormity of his own crime. Indeed, the "golden rule" of supposing yourself to change places with your neighbour, and reflecting what you would then think it right for him to do towards you, is merely an admonition to employ in one (very numerous) class of cases, such a mode of reasoning.

In every employment of what may be called ["fictitious," or] "invented example" [reasoning from a supposed case], the argument will manifestly have no weight, unless the result that is supposed in the imaginary case, be such as one would fully *anticipate*.

On the other hand, *real* instances have weight, even though they be such as one would not have *expected*. For instance, that all animals with horns on the head should chew the cud, and should be destitute of upper cutting-teeth, is what no one would have originally *conjectured;* but extensive observation has so fully established this as a

universal rule, that a naturalist, on findi:
of some unknown animal with horns on 1
at once pronounce it a ruminant, and w
of the absence of upper incisors.

§ 15. When an Argument of the Clas
[from Example, Analogy, &c.] is *opposed*
of the Premises, it is usual, in ordinary c
either, "the statement is *not correct*," w
the *Minor*-premise,—or "this case does n
"not in *point*,"]—or "does not *hold good*
the one before us;" or "the cases are *not*
amounts (as you will see on examination
Major-premise.

Thus, if any one recommends to his ;
medicine, as having been found service
Typhus, it might be either denied that
viceable in those cases (which would be
Minor,) or again it might be denied th:
disorder is the *same* as those; which w
of the *Major*-premise.

And here observe, that two things ma
in most respects, and yet quite alike—i
may hold good—in the one point that is
argument : or, again, they may disagr
though they are analogous in many othe1

And it is from inattention to this disti
arguments from Analogy are often reje
cious ones admitted.

§ 16. For instance, in the Parables a
if a man should object that "a lamb is
thing from a wife," and "a ship, from ε
differences, every one would see, do
Analogy in question.

On the other hand, there is an Anal
spects between all " valuable Articles" th
corn and iron or lead, and again (what
precious metals) gold and silver.   And
supply of *most* of these articles, while
price, would not-diminish their *usefulness*
prove a general benefit, some might infer
hold good in respect of gold and silver.

If the earth should yield two bushels of corn, or two tons of iron or lead, for one that it now yields, these articles would be much cheaper; while a bushel of corn would be as useful in feeding us, as now; and so with most other articles.

But if the supply of gold or silver were thus doubled, the chief *use* of these being for *coin*, and the *utility* of coin *depending on its value*, the only important change would be that a sovereign or a shilling would be twice as large as now; and therefore twice as cumbrous. So that no advantage would result.

It is manifest that in a train of Reasoning, it will often happen that several of the different kinds of argument we have spoken of will be combined. Thus we may perhaps have to prove by several Examples, the existence of a certain "Cause;" and from that cause to infer a certain "Effect;" and that effect again may be employed as a "Sign" to infer a certain "Condition," &c.

In this, and the preceding Lessons, several interesting subjects have been very slightly touched on, which may be found more fully treated of, and the views now taken more developed, in treatises on those several subjects.*

If you proceed, in following up this course of study, to peruse such treatises, you will have been prepared, it is hoped, to find that perusal the easier and the more interesting, from what has been explained in these Lessons : and you will be the better able to understand what is valuable, in other works on such subjects, and to detect anything that may be erroneous.

---

* In the *Elements of Rhetoric*, Part L, the subjects of this last Lesson are more fully treated of.

www.ingramcontent.com/pod-product-compliance
Lightning Source LLC
Chambersburg PA
CBHW021134020726
47500CB00003B/1070